IN THUG LOVE WITH A CHI-TOWN MILLIONAIRE 3

J. DOMINIQUE

In Thug Love With A Chi-Town Millionaire 3

Copyright © 2022 by J. Dominique

All rights reserved.

Published in the United States of America.

Published by Cole Hart Signature, LLC.

Mailing List

To stay up to date on new releases, plus get information on contests, sneak peeks, and more,

Go To The Website Below...

www.colehartsignature.com

CASH

I instantly hopped out of my chair and pulled my phone out to call Camille as anger coursed through me. Even if this was a joke, it was far from funny, and just the implication that my son was in harm's way had me seeing red. I could give a fuck less about Vernique but my son, I'd go to war behind him.

"Oh, you wanna die, huh? Who the fuck is this?" I asked, growing more pissed when Camille still hadn't answered her phone. Switching gears, I dialed Lou and his shit just rang until the voicemail picked up.

"Awww, listen at Baby Banks tryna sound tough. If you want yo' kid back you're gonna have to come out yo' pockets tho'. How much you think this lil' muhfucka worth, Nique? I'd say the heir to the Banks's throne is worth at least a quarter mil'. Matter fact, I shouldn't even shortchange myself like that. Let's just gone head and round that up to say, five hundred thousand. That's a nice number." This nigga had the nerve to laugh in my ear. I wanted so bad to tell his ass to suck my dick, but the fact that I couldn't reach Camille or Lou told me there was some truth to what he was saying. My pops

and Dinero were now huddled around me looking concerned, but I was too focused on the bitch nigga in my ear.

"Ayite, but I need to know Kash is straight. Let me talk to him, put him on the phone," I demanded, even though some of the bass left my voice. My son was my heart and if anything happened to him because of this street shit, then I'd be fucked up. This was the shit Camille had been talking about, and I'd been so confident that I had everything under control and now some nigga had snatched up my son.

I heard him shuffling around a little before Kash's crying became loud and prominent, and I pressed the phone harder to my ear. Dude was definitely going to die for this stunt, but if he hurt my son then I'd make sure to torture him first. "Aye, say hey to yo' daddy."

"Daaaaddy!"

"Kash! Kash!" I called frantically.

"Ahhh, listen at you. Kash! Kash! You sound like a bitch!" he laughed, and my jaw clenched tightly. I already couldn't wait to kill this nigga. "Ayite look, I'ma call you back with a location for you to bring my money. Stay by the phone!" The three beeps let me know his bitch ass had hung up, and now everybody was surrounding me asking questions.

"I gotta go to the crib, somethin' might be wrong with Camille." I was handing my mama her phone back and about to leave, but Ca'Mahri jumped right in my way.

"What you mean something's wrong with my sister? What happened to Camille!" she yelled, moving with me as I tried to go around her.

"I don't know, I'm goin' to see now, Cam." I tried to keep my voice calm so she wouldn't get any more worked up, but that shit didn't help at all. Looking at Dinero, I motioned for him to help and he finally jumped into action, grabbing her shoulders and telling her to calm down.

"No! If my sister's in trouble then I'm goin' too!"

"Give me yo' keys, bro."

"What's goin' on, Cash? Where's Camille and my grandbaby!" Now both women were going off as Dinero fished out his keys and handed them off to me.

"Nah, y'all go check that shit out together, I got them," my pops ordered, snatching up both Ca'Mahri and our mama. Neither of them were a match for his buff ass, and it gave us time to leave. Since I still had the keys, I jumped in the driver's seat and pulled off while I filled Dinero in on what I knew.

"What the hell? This shit crazy, man." His face balled up once I finished. "You think this shit random? What if it's Lox weird ass? We still ain't found that nigga."

"How the hell Vernique know his ass though?" I didn't know what to think. We hadn't had any other issues out of Lox since he robbed the trap. Had his ass really just popped back up out of nowhere, and with my baby mama of all people? If Vernique had anything to do with this shit, she was going to die right along with that nigga, and I didn't give a fuck that she was Kash's mother. Hell, she didn't!

Dinero was still talking, but I wasn't paying his ass any attention as we pulled up at home and saw the gate sitting wide open. I could see up ahead where Lou's car sat with the brake lights glowing, and my heart pounded in my chest. This whole time I'd just been trying to get to Camille, but pulling up and seeing the scene before me filled me with dread. I was almost afraid to look, but I kept driving until I stopped in front of my house. The front door was wide open and I could clearly see Lou's big ass laid out right in front of it. There was really no point in even checking him because the pool of blood pouring out of his head let me know he was gone. I shared a look with Dinero and rushed inside, frantically searching for Camille. I saw her feet first and instantly my heart dropped as I ran over to her. The lights *flicked on, so I was able to see, and I quickly inspected her body, not seeing any visible gunshots. She did, however, have a big ass knot on her forehead.*

"Camille! Camille, baby, get up!" I lifted her body in my arms and grabbed her face, giving it a few light slaps.

"Hmm." Moaning, she came to and squinted as her eyes tried to adjust to the light. "Kash, where's Kash?" she questioned weakly, trying to sit up but fell back against me right as Dinero returned and shook his head, letting me know Kash really wasn't there.

"Fuck! Baby, I need to take you to the hospital. You might have a concussion." Camille was still looking confused as I lifted her in my arms bridal style and carried her to the car. My brother followed behind me and put in a call to the cleanup crew.

After I got Camille settled across the backseat, I climbed in with her and Dinero drove us right back to the hospital. Shorty was crying the whole way and trying to explain what happened but, aside from Lou getting killed and her being knocked out, she didn't know shit. She didn't even mention Vernique, just a nigga dressed in dark clothes.

"It's okay, bae, I got you now, but you can't tell these muhfuckas none of that. You gone have to tell them you tripped or some shit, but please do not tell them what you just told me." I stared down into her face to make sure she understood me. The last thing we needed was the police sniffing around and asking questions. I wanted full control over how this shit ended. She gave a slight nod as we pulled up to the hospital, and I carried her inside.

"Aye, I need some help over here. My girl pregnant and she's hurt!" That drew the attention of everybody in the emergency room, and they quickly came out with a stretcher. A nurse directed me to the waiting area as they wheeled her back, and my jaw clenched irritably. I didn't like that they didn't want to let me back for something as simple as a head injury when Camille was pregnant with my baby, but I wasn't going to trip. Instead, I made my way over to

my family with my brother, and as soon as Ca'Mahri saw us she jumped up with questions.

"Where's Camille? What happened to my sister, Cash?" Sighing, I dropped into a chair and rested my head in my hands.

"She's in the back gettin' looked at. A muhfucka knocked her out, but other than that she's fine."

"Somebody did what? She ain't fine if somebody put their hands on her, she's pregnant!"

After all the shit I was dealing with, the last thing I was trying to do was listen to Ca'Mahri yelling. I could definitely understand her concern because if it was my brother I would've been ready to blow some shit up. Unfortunately, it wasn't just about Camille and the baby. My son was in danger and my fucking granny was fighting for her life. It was a lot going on, and all I wanted her ass to do was get out of my face so I could think.

"Bro, please. I ain't tryna get disrespectful, so get yo' girl and let her know what the fuck goin' on, man." I gave Dinero a look that let him know we'd be in that bitch tearing it up if she didn't take her ass on somewhere. I already knew how he was and as soon as I turned up on her he'd be ready to fight, and tonight I was with all the bullshit.

"Get me—"

"Bae, come here, man." He pulled her away, and I breathed a sigh of relief as my pops came over with my mama right on his heels. They were clearly expecting answers and aside from Kash being gone and Camille being hurt in the process, I didn't have shit to tell them.

My mama immediately burst into tears, and he put his arm around her, looking just as fucked up as me. He was having to worry about his own mama and his grandson at the same time. We weren't used to shit like this, and the fact that we couldn't do shit but wait was eating away at us.

"Uhhh, family of Dorothea Harris!" As soon as we heard my

granny's name, we all surrounded the doctor who looked stale in the face, and it instantly pissed me off. He didn't seem moved one way or another, so I couldn't even tell if I should've been hopeful or not.

"That's us. How's my mama doin'?" The pain was evident in my pops's voice, but that did little to change dude's crusty ass demeanor. Nodding, he looked over all of us with his beady blue eyes and then ducked his head into the clipboard he was holding.

"Okay, well, Ms. Harris suffered a severe myocardial infarction and—"

"Hold up, nigga, what? Use English, my guy!" I instantly cut in with my face balled up.

"It's um, it's a heart attack," he stammered, looking around at us like we were slow. I resisted the urge to hem his stupid ass up as he continued talking. "We were able to get her heart restarted, but the time without oxygen to the brain does take a toll on the body. She's stable, but she is comatose and hooked up to life support."

Anything else that nigga said faded out, and all I could see was red. My granny on life support, my girl being hurt, and my son being in the wind all were enough to turn me into a whole demon. Niggas definitely weren't ready for the type of havoc I was about to cause.....

To be continued

CHAPTER ONE
CA'MAHRI

Before the doctor could finish informing us on Ms. Dorothea's condition, Cash tossed a chair across the room and angrily stormed out. The outburst had his mama calling his name sternly, but he didn't turn around.

"I got him, Ma," Dinero sighed, giving her hand a quick squeeze before running after him. Once he was out of the room the doctor slowly picked back up where he'd left off while I hugged myself and tried to blink back my tears.

"Like I was saying, she is stable and we're doing everything we can to keep her as comfortable as possible." Just from the way he paused, I knew that he was on the verge of saying something that was going to make the situation worse. I braced myself as he grimaced and shifted his steel blue eyes across the room, before looking back at Mr. Kendrick. "When dealing with situations like this, I always advise the family to uh... start making preparations just in ca—"

"You bet not fix them nonexistent lips to advise me shit 'bout burying my muthafuckin' mama!" Mr. Kendrick thundered, snatching out of his wife's grip and stepping into the doctor's face. "If you value your life, you're gonna do everything you can to make sure Dorothea Banks walks up out this bitch!"

"I, um," the man stammered, turning white as a ghost as he retreated and looked to me and Ms. Keisha for help, but I damn sure wasn't about to jump my little ass in the line of fire for him. It was obvious that Mr. Kendrick was just as unhinged as his sons, and I wanted no parts of that shit.

"Kendrick, baby, please just calm down before you get put out and they don't let us see her." Ms. Keisha tucked herself into his side and placed a hand on his chest to calm him, but her words only had his face twisting up even more.

"I wish the fuck they would! Let me see my mama right god damn now!" The bass in his voice had the doctor nodding quickly and mumbling for them to follow him. I watched them disappear behind the double doors and silently prayed that his ass didn't say something else that would cause Mr. Kendrick to make good on his threat.

"Are you Ca'Mahri?" At the sound of my name, I turned to see a nurse standing next to me and my brows knotted in confusion.

"Yeeeah?" I dragged, and relief flashed across her face.

"Okay, your sister is up and asking for you."

I'd completely forgotten about Camille being brought into the emergency room after the commotion surrounding Ms. Dorothea, but I hurriedly went to follow her to the back. She filled me in on the little bit she did know as we made our way to Camille's room, and I attempted to keep my attitude in check. Apparently, she'd been attacked and hit across the head in the short amount of time between her leaving and being carried back in by Cash. I was pissed just hearing that shit, but when I laid eyes on her, I was ready to blow the whole damn hospital up. Already she had a knot the size of a golf ball on her forehead, and I wondered what the hell she'd been hit with.

"Oh hell naw, what the fuck happened to you?" I shrieked angrily as I stopped at her bedside with tears stinging my eyes. I wasn't used to seeing my sister look anything less than perfect, even after throwing hands with a bitch, so to see her in a hospital bed lumped up and knowing she was pregnant had me pissed off.

"I fell on Cash's steps," she said flatly, and I cocked my head, not trying to hide my confusion.

"But Cash said——"

"Can I have some water please?" she interrupted, giving me a look before cutting her eyes to the nurse.

"Oh, I'm sorry. Yes, I'll go get that right away and the doctor will be in with you shortly." She rushed off and Camille kept her eyes on her until she was sure the lady was gone.

"Girl, she's gone, now what the hell happened?" At this point I was getting impatient as hell and wasn't trying to wait on her slow ass anymore.

"I don't know. One minute we were walkin' into the house and the next, Lou's fuckin' head was gettin' blown off, then some nigga walked in and knocked me out. By the time I came to, Cash and Dinero were there and baby Kash was gone!" she sobbed, and my hands instantly covered my mouth in shock. Once I recovered, I quickly wrapped her up in a hug and tried to comfort her, knowing that she had to be torn up behind this shit. When Cash said somebody knocked her out, I'd been thinking she'd gotten into it with his baby mama again or something, not that she was involved in a whole murder and kidnapping. It was obvious that whatever was going on had something to do with the Banks men, and I was shook as fuck. Despite knowing they were in the streets heavy, I'd never been directly affected by that shit and neither had Camille that I was aware of. The fact that the fortress they called a home had been infiltrated and their security was killed in front of my sister was too much and had me rethinking shit. As hood as we were having grown up in Chicago where shooting was an everyday occurrence, I still didn't feel equipped to be in a serious relationship with a nigga so deep in the streets.

My sister was lucky as hell to be walking away with just a knot on her forehead considering all that she'd been through, and I didn't want to release the hold I had on her, just knowing how close I'd come to possibly not having her anymore.

"I just feel so fuckin' bad. That crazy muthafucka could be doin' anything to that baby right now! Cash ain't never gone forgive me if something happens to him!" she continued to bawl, and I fought the urge to tell her fuck Cash! I understood he was probably going through it after what happened to Ms. Dorothea and Kash being snatched up the same night, but he'd be a fool to blame this shit on my sister! Before I could tell her that, there was a knock at the door and in stepped the doctor with the nurse right on her heels, carrying the water that Camille had requested.

"Oh no, don't cry, honey!" The smile that was on her face immediately fell as she came further into the room and stopped on the other side of Camille. "I'm sure the baby's just fine, don't you even worry. I'm Dr. Kelly and I'll be checking you out today," she cooed soothingly as she rubbed small circles on Camille's back. I moved over slightly so the nurse could hand over her water, but was still close enough that she could hold my hand while the doctor asked her questions and looked her over.

"Well, you seem to be just fine besides the swelling, but since it's on your head I'm still going to order an MRI to be on the safe side. As far as the little one, they've got a good strong heartbeat and don't seem to be in distress." Dr. Kelly smiled warmly and hung her stethoscope back around her neck. I could visibly see the relief flash across Camille's face hearing that the baby was doing okay, and after letting us know that someone would be in shortly to wheel her down to the MRI machine, they disappeared from the room.

They didn't lie either, because not even ten minutes later a completely different nurse glided in and helped Camille into a wheelchair. We didn't have far to travel, and within a half hour she was receiving her discharge papers with a clean bill of health.

I wheeled her back out to the waiting area to see if Cash was still out there since he'd disappeared after the news about Ms. Dorothea, but the only one out there was Dinero. As soon as he saw us he was on his feet, and I questioned him with my eyes about Cash, right as Camille did.

"Where's your brother? Did y'all find out anything about Kash? Oh damn, is Ms. Dorothea okay?" she fired off question after question without giving him a chance to respond before asking another, and I could tell from the look on his face that he didn't have good news for her. Our eyes met briefly before he focused on her with a sigh.

"Uhh, Cash went to follow up on a couple of leads, but as far as my grandma, they got her stable and my pops and OG up there with her now. How's my lil' niece or nephew doin'? Y'all straight?" A brief smile crossed her face at the mention of the baby, masking the hurt that she'd tried to blink away, and I gave her shoulder an encouraging squeeze. Hearing that Cash had left the building without at least checking on her probably wasn't easy to stomach, but her concern for Kash outweighed everything else at the moment.

"We're okay, I just....I'm worried about Kash." Her voice cracked.

"Don't stress yourself out, sis, me and bro got everybody

combing the streets for him. We gone get him back, ayite." His confidence had her releasing the tension in her shoulders just slightly.

"I'm about to schedule us a ride to Camille's so she can rest. I know you probably wanna stay and check on Ms. Dorothea or catch up with Cash," I said, instantly avoiding the hard glare he sent my way. I was hoping that he wouldn't put up a fight considering everything that was going on, but the way his jaw clenched let me know that's exactly what he was going to do. He was already shaking his head emphatically and moving into my personal space.

"No, Camille's crib is out of the question, and I definitely ain't lettin' y'all ass get in an Uber. Hell naw!" I opened my mouth to object but he quickly cut me off.

"But—"

"Ain't even no point in tryna argue. I understand the estate probably don't feel the most secure right now, but that nigga only got lucky 'cause we were focused on my granny. Trust me, ain't nobody else gettin' in that bitch though. That's on my soul! Besides, we got the full security team there now. Camille can come back to our crib, it's plenty of guest rooms she can pick from. Matter fact, y'all can just go to the penthouse."

"That'd make me feel better if it wasn't for the fact that my sister had security with her when this shit happened," I sassed with a hand on my hip. As protective as he was over his family, I was too when it came to my sister. She'd gotten hurt on their property, and whether he wanted to accept it or not, it was because of some shit they were into.

Instead of responding, he let out a bitter chuckle as he fished his phone out and pressed it to his ear like we weren't in the middle of a conversation. There were times when that cocky shit was a complete turn on, but at the moment, it didn't do anything but irritate me more. All I wanted was a little time to think, maybe weigh my options about our relationship, and he was being his usual bossy self.

"See, it's settled. I already got a car outside for y'all. Come on." He was off the phone and already moving to grab the handles of Camille's chair. Rolling my eyes hard, I followed behind him since there was no sense in trying to argue. It was late and the excitement of the day had me too tired, but once I got some rest I'd be ready for round two.

CHAPTER TWO
DINERO

As soon as I made sure Ca'Mahri and Camille were safely in the truck with the armed security and headed home, I made my way over to my car so I could catch up to Cash. He'd gone to see if Mason, our tech guy, could do some type of trace on Vernique's phone. As soon as I was behind the wheel, I dialed him right up.

"Did he find anything yet?" I asked before he could even greet me.

"Nigga, I just got here," he huffed, and on cue, I could hear his car door slamming as he got out. "You bouta be on your way?"

"Yeah, I just sent Cam and Camille to the crib and I'm leavin' out now." I maneuvered through the parking lot and pulled out, blending into the flow of traffic. At the mention of Camille he cursed and then the line fell silent.

"Shit, I forgot all about her being up there. Her and the baby straight though, right?" Even though he was trying to play it cool, his voice still gave away his guilt about forgetting she was in the emergency room. I hadn't really asked for any details, but them not keeping her overnight had to mean she was okay, which was what I told him.

"I mean, shit, they let her go home. All Ca'Mahri really said was that she was tryna take her to get some rest. She do seem real fucked up behind Kash tho'. Her ass was bouta cry just askin' 'bout him," I said, and my jaw clenched thinking about my nephew. Her reaction let me know she felt guilty about what happened, but no one was to blame besides that nigga Lox, and I was going to make sure he paid for his violation.

"Maaaan, let me call and check on her right quick. I'ma see you when you get here."

"Ayite, bet."

As soon as we hung up, a text came through from the cleanup crew saying that they'd finished back at Cash's crib. There hadn't really been much to do besides clearing out Lou's body from the porch, but I gave them instructions to take him to the funeral home so we could bury him the right way. Lou deserved a proper burial, and I was going to make sure to look out for his family too.

It didn't take me long to get to Mason's crib. I parked right behind Cash before making the short trip up to his door. Lifting my fist, I prepared to knock, but Cash swung it open and then walked off with his phone pressed against his ear. From his tone I could tell he was still talking to Camille, as I locked up and followed him further into the house. While Cash ducked off into the living room I continued on to where I knew Mason was. His office was on the first floor right off the kitchen, and when I walked inside he was typing away furiously on his keyboard. Dropping into the chair next to him, I eyed the three computer screens, unable to recognize anything that was displayed. He real life had that shit set up like he was Batman or somebody, and it always seemed like it was something new in there whenever I came over.

"What's good, D?" he asked, never taking his eyes off the screen.

"A bunch of bullshit, but what else is new, right?" Sighing, I leaned forward like a closer look would help me to figure out what I was looking at. "What's all this though?"

"Right now I'm hacking into her phone's system so I can gain access to her location. Fuckin' around with Apple, it might take a while though." He shrugged just as Cash came back into the room.

"Camille cool?" I lifted a brow at him as he stood behind Mason with his arms folded, causing him to scoff.

"Yeah man, she was just tryna convince me to let her come help look for Kash. She better lay her pregnant ass down some-where and put some ice on that fuckin' hickey on her head!" he fumed. I just shook my head at his crazy ass and pulled my vibrating phone from my pocket. The way he was talking, I half expected for it to be Ca'Mahri calling to further plead her sister's case, but it was just a text from the security checking in. I wasn't taking any chances this time and had told them to hit me up every half hour while I handled business with Cash.

"She feel bad about that shit, plus she probably trauma-tized as fuck after what happened to Lou." I had my head buried in my phone as I quickly navigated to my text thread with Ca'Mahri. She probably didn't think I noticed the look of doubt in her eyes back at the hospital, but I was all too familiar with it. Both Tania and Asha had looked at me that exact same way before they'd distanced themselves from me. That's why I immediately put a stop to her going to Camille's crib. I wasn't going to let her walk away from me that easily, especially not in the middle of a crisis.

"The fuck she feel guilty for? This was Lou's fuck up! His big ass should've been payin' attention, that's what he was gettin' paid for!"

"I mean, *we* know that, but the girls ain't used to this shit so they don't," I reasoned, as I sent Ca'Mahri a text asking if she was okay. Almost immediately, the little bubbles popped up and either she was writing out a long ass paragraph or she was trying to think of how to respond, both of which had me slightly nervous.

"No, no, no, no, noooo! Shit!" My head shot up at Mason's outburst as he angrily slammed his fist on the desk.

"What the fuck happened? What's wrong?" Cash was immediately standing right next to him, looking between the three screens frantically.

"He cut the phone off! I don't know if he just got a hunch we were tracking them or what, but I can't do anything if the phone's powered off!" Dejectedly, he pushed away from the desk and slumped down in his chair.

"Fuck it, we movin' on to plan B. You still got that nigga info?" Cash questioned, and Mason bobbed his head before pulling a folder out from under the desk and handing it to him. "Ayite, keep trying the phone for now. He gotta call for the money so hopefully he'll cut it back on. Come on, bro." He nodded for me and was on his way out the door before I could even stand up. I really didn't know what his crazy ass had in mind, but I was right behind him.

"Look, we shuttin' everything down until I find out where the fuck my son at, so if you wanna eat, then get us a fuckin' lead!" Cash's plan B was to call every one of our workers, from the corner boys to the lieutenants, for a last-minute meeting, and threatening them. Immediately, I was against that shit. The last thing we needed to do was slow down the money considering that Tino had already warned us. I wanted to find my nephew just as bad as everyone else, but if Tino got involved, we'd fuck around and not even be alive to find him. Immediately, a chorus of grumbles erupted around the room, letting me know our workers weren't happy about the news, and I released a sigh. "You muhfuckas got some shit to say? Spit that shit out then!"

"We ain't got no problem findin' lil' Kash, but we still need to be making some type of money in the meantime," a nigga named Squeak spoke up in a trembling voice, drawing all eyes to him. "I mean, we don't know how long this shit gone take....what if we don't never—"

Before he could finish the rest of that stupid ass sentence, Cash shot him in the throat, splashing blood on everybody near him. They all jumped back and watched as he fell to the ground clutching his neck.

"Anybody else wanna die tonight, say some dumb shit like what that nigga was 'bout to!" Cash grit, looking over the room with murderous eyes. "Matter fact, I don't even wanna hear shit else. Starting tonight, half y'all niggas need to be in Milwaukee checking every relative on file and the other half need to be here, and I don't give a fuck if y'all gotta go door to door with my man's picture, but I want him found!"

This time when he spoke there was complete silence because them niggas didn't want to say shit that could possibly get their heads blown off. Tucking his gun away, he turned to me. "Bro, you gone stay here with the Chicago group and I'ma ride out to Milwaukee with the others so—"

"Hell naw, I'm goin' where you goin'!" I quickly stopped him. It was one thing to let him make some decisions, but I wasn't about to send his ass after Lox alone. As his big brother and Kash's uncle, I wouldn't feel right letting him go without me as backup. I was already on my feet ready to plead my case, when my father's voice came booming through the warehouse.

"He's right, your brother needs to go with you and I can handle the search here." Our pops came through the crowd of men already dressed down in all black. Being the legend he was, every man in attendance was looking on in awe. Only some of them had been inherited from his team, so it was really the first time that a lot of them had ever seen him in the flesh and ready to put in work.

"Pop's—" Cash started, but he put a hand up stopping him, shaking his head firmly.

"I'm good, just tell me who you want with me so we can go find my grandson."

With a slight nod Cash did exactly what he told him, and split the men so that my pops had a majority of them since I was going with him. Our father might have been sure about being back out in the field, but neither of us were taking any chances when it came to his old ass. We already had a serious scare with our grandma, it wasn't no way we were risking his ass too. After we had that taken care of we all headed out so everybody could get their home situation taken care of before we got on the road, and I tried to prepare myself to face Ca'Mahri.

CHAPTER THREE
CAMILLE

I paced the room waiting on another call from Cash, and damn near jumped at the sound of a knock on the door. Ca'Mahri peeked her head in and I breathed a sigh of relief, even though my heart was still pounding out of my chest.

"Camille, what you doin' out of bed? You need to be restin'!" she huffed, rushing inside, and I rolled my eyes irritably as she ushered me back to the bed.

"Girl, I got a knot on my head I'm not a damn invalid!" I wasn't trying to take my frustrations out on her, but she'd been doing the most ever since she stepped into my hospital room. If I'd let her, she would straight up have been treating me like one of the elderly people she worked with at the nursing home.

"Okay, and in addition to that you're pregnant with my niece or nephew and been through a traumatic experience. So, if I wanna baby yo' black ass then that's what I'm gone do!" she shot right back, completely unbothered by my attitude.

"I'm sorry, I just haven't heard from Cash and that shit

making me even more worried." My voice cracked as another set of tears threatened to erupt. I didn't know if it was the pregnancy making me so much more emotional about things or what, but I had been crying on and off ever since I'd left the hospital. It didn't help that it had been hours since I'd last talked to Cash. I needed an update on both him and Kash, and the longer I went without one the more my stress elevated.

A sympathetic look covered Ca'Mahri's face and she wrapped her arm around me, resting her head on my shoulder. "Don't worry, I'm sure he's gonna be bustin' his rude ass in here any minute with some good news." I gave her a small smile even though I was filled with doubt, just as the door was pushed open by none other than Cash himself. My heart fluttered as I studied every inch of him, trying to gauge his mood, and came up empty. He looked back at me through low red eyes that were completely void of emotion, and all I wanted to do was hold him. Without speaking, I was up and in his arms, releasing a breath I didn't know I was holding.

"Ayite, I'ma head out and give y'all some privacy." Ca'Mahri was already shuffling to the door.

"Aw yeah, bro need to holla at you," Cash tossed out, and despite me being totally wrapped up in the sea of emotions I was feeling, I distinctly heard her suck her teeth before she closed the door. I made a mental note to ask her about it later because at the moment all I could worry about was the man before me. I don't know how long we stood there silently embracing before I worked up the courage to speak.

"Baby, I'm so, so—"

"Nah, don't even say that shit again. I already told you this shit ain't yo' fault so stop apologizing," he cut me off sternly, and I tried to suck up the tears that were already spilling down my cheeks.

"But—"

"Ain't no buts." He pulled away just enough to look down into my face, and once he saw the wetness there his eyes softened as he thumbed my tears away. "You gotta chill, baby, none of this shit is your fault and I'm not tryna be worried about you and my baby while I'm gone."

His constant reassurance should've made me feel better, but it didn't. In the midst of a crisis, I'd panicked and was unable to defend myself or Kash. Hell, I wasn't even able to run once I saw that we were in danger, and the guilt of it all was eating me alive. I didn't want to be the reason he was distracted, though, worrying about me, so I held back the urge to argue my point and simply nodded.

"Ayite?"

"Alright," I agreed, forcing a small smile to try and put him at ease, but the tension in his body was still there despite his expression softening just slightly.

"Good, now come feed my baby so I can make sure you're in bed resting like the doctor told you before I leave." Quickly pecking my lips, he intertwined his fingers with mine and started toward the door. I couldn't lie, hearing that he was about to leave me when he'd only just gotten back had my chest tight. The last thing I wanted was to be away from him, but I knew he needed to go out and find Kash, so I shook off the urge to say anything and followed him out to Dinero's kitchen.

I didn't have a clue what he'd brought, but whatever it was had my mouth watering before we even made it to the table. Food hadn't been on my mind at all this entire time, but suddenly my stomach felt like it was touching my back. Cash wasted no time pulling out a chair for me and I dropped into it, ready to dig in.

"Mmmmm." I ignored the knowing look on his face as he set out two Styrofoam trays. Opening the first one, I was met with four perfectly fried pieces of catfish, some spaghetti, and green beans, and in the other tray was a huge helping of peach cobbler. I'd already started working on my first piece of greasy, fried goodness when he held out a plastic fork.

"That shit good, huh?" He sat down next to me with his arm stretched across the back of my chair. Since my mouth was full and I didn't want to stop eating, I nodded vigorously, causing a hint of a smile to cross his lips. "Mmhmm, baby daddy got the hook up." He winked.

I continued eating while he basically just watched and caressed my lower back. Between the food and comfort of having him so close, I was in pregnancy heaven, but it wasn't long before I'd completely finished both trays and sadness quickly filled me.

"Come on so I can tuck yo' fine ass in," he teased, kissing the corner of my mouth and helping me up. "And my baby bet not have a stomachache after the way you just vacuumed that shit up neither." Like the true sour patch kid he was, he had to say something smart after having been so sweet, and I sucked my teeth.

"You're the one who bought it for me, but trust me, yo' mean ass baby will be just fine." Waving him off, I started back toward the bedroom and he wasn't too far behind me. With ease he caught up, wrapping his arms around my waist from behind and matching my steps.

"'Cause I knew you was too busy worrying to eat, but I didn't think yo' greedy ass was gon' eat it all."

"That's what you get for thinkin' you know so much," I said, making faces as we entered the room.

"Maaaan, just get in the bed, bruh," he ordered, and despite me poking my lip out I was actually tired as hell. My body sank into the plush mattress and my eyes involuntarily lowered. I hadn't noticed how comfortable it was when I'd laid down before, but with Cash there and a full belly, I was able to fully enjoy it. No doubt Dinero hadn't spared any expense on the cloud-like mattress, and I was very appreciative. Cash had a pretty comfortable bed too but after what happened, I didn't think I'd ever be able to step foot inside his house again, let alone his bedroom. That was the least of our worries though.

Without a word, Cash climbed in next to me, folding his arms behind his head, and I snuggled up against him with a yawn. "I thought you were leaving."

"I got a few minutes before we gotta jump on the highway, I just wanna make sure you're good before I go." He sounded just as tired as me, but I knew he wasn't going to rest until Kash was found. Pressing tighter against him and laying my leg over his, I relaxed and fell into a light sleep.

It felt like I'd just closed my eyes when I was jolted awake by a loud noise, and I realized I'd only been asleep for twenty minutes. The next thing I noticed was Cash's empty side of the bed, and I instantly panicked. Without thinking, I jumped to my feet, ignoring the slight throbbing in my temple, and looked around for the nearest weapon, which just so happened to be a heavy ass glass vase from the nightstand. Last time I had been caught off guard, but this time I was going to make sure I fucked somebody up.

I psyched myself up and slowly pulled the door open, hoping that whoever was out there wouldn't hear me. Just as I was about to step out, though, Cash's unmistakable voice along with Ca'Mahri and Dinero stopped me in my tracks, and I breathed a sigh of relief until I listened to their conversation.

"Y'all muhfuckas really tryna do this shit like right now when we need to be findin' my son?" Cash questioned, making my brows snap together.

"I'm good, I been told him y'all can go." The tone of my sister's voice was one I'd heard before when a nigga had fucked up with her, and I thought about how she'd seemed annoyed by Dinero's presence when they'd first arrived. Whatever he'd done had to have her heated if she didn't even want to wait until they got Kash back to bring it up.

"You know what, fuck it. You right, bro, we need to handle this other shit right now, but *we will* finish this when I get back."

"Ain't nothin' to finish, I already told you I'm good," Ca'Mahri said dismissively, and I finally made my presence known. All eyes landed on me, but my sister and Dinero both immediately turned their hard stares back on each other until he scoffed and gave his attention to Cash.

"I'ma meet you in the car, man, hurry up and go say bye to Camille." With that he stalked off, making sure to slam the door. As soon as he was gone, Cash scratched the back of his neck and sighed, clearly uncomfortable with the tension still lingering in the room.

"Cam, you straight—"

"Juuuust fuckin' perfect," she cut him off with a snort and disappeared into the other room, also slamming the door shut.

"What the fuck that nigga do to my sister?" I huffed, shuffling across the room to meet him.

"Man, just give me a kiss so I can go before this nigga leave me. You already know her ass gon' fill you in once I'm gone." I couldn't even talk shit because I knew he was right. Even if Ca'Mahri didn't want to tell me, I was going to force it out of her. Stepping into his outstretched arms, I hugged him extra tight and puckered my lips for a kiss. I wasn't ready for him to leave me yet, but I kept that to myself.

"I love you," I told him breathily, unable to keep the emotion out of my voice. "So make sure you come back to me and don't come home without Kash."

"I'ma always find my way back to you 'cause I love yo' bean

head ass too, and my mans gone be right with me." The fact that I wholeheartedly believed him made it easier to release my hold, and after another quick kiss he was gone. I said a silent prayer for all of their safety before going to find out what I'd missed during my cat nap.

CHAPTER FOUR

LOX

"I want my daddy!" the little nigga Kash whined for what felt like the hundredth time, and I rolled my eyes. I wasn't used to being around kids and after this shit, I wasn't trying to ever be again. All the little fucker did was whine, and after a week of the shit I was ready to take my belt off and give him the ass whooping his *daddy* never did. This ransom shit had seemed like a good idea when Vernique first asked for my help getting her shorty back. I could kill two birds with one stone by shaking that nigga Cash up and getting some money out the deal.

The problem was that I couldn't decide the best way to do the exchange without me ending up dead. There was no point in trying to get money if I wasn't alive to spend the shit. I couldn't think, though, with Vernique and her son constantly in my ear either crying, complaining, or both.

"Aye man, shut that lil' nigga up!" I growled, enjoying the fear that flashed across her face. After seeing me murk that nigga back at Cash's crib she knew not to try me, which was good because I wouldn't have no problem offing her ass too. At this point she was only alive to care for her son since I didn't have no use for her. I damn sure wasn't splitting my money with her ass! I was a greedy nigga. Shit, growing up in the foster care system had a way of making you selfish as fuck, and I was definitely a product of my environment. Born addicted to crack by a bitch who didn't even stick around at the hospital, I'd only had myself to depend on for as long as I could remember. It wasn't until I was twelve that I was finally placed with Rhonda Moore's old ass. That's where I'd met Walt. She had five boys there but the others were way younger than us, so Walt rode my coat tails hard. As soon as he saw me stand up to the niggas on the block that were constantly beating his ass, he glorified me and stayed tagging along whenever I left the house. He thought we were bonding and shit, but the whole time I was really making his ass do bad shit for entertainment, like steal or snatch purses on Michigan Street. If he got caught he was always on his own, but if he managed to bring back anything, I'd leave his ass the scraps. Wasn't no splitting shit down the middle. He'd always been a send off and was only as important to me as what I could get out of him. That's why when I heard of his death it didn't faze me at all. It was like Camron said in *Paid in Full*, niggas get shot every day.

Crash!

"No! I said no!"

I snapped out of my daze to see his ass had thrown my fucking remote, sending a glass picture frame crashing to the floor in pieces. He was having a whole fucking tantrum and making my eye twitch. Without thinking, I was up and across the room in a flash and snatching him out of her lap by the arm.

"Lox—!" The murderous look I shot Vernique instantly shut her up and she swallowed hard, pleading with me with her eyes, but that didn't faze me at all. Turning my attention back to Kash, who'd stopped yelling as tears streaked down his face, I gave him a couple of shakes.

"Sit yo' lil' ass down somewhere and shut up before I make sure you never see yo' daddy again, you understand?" I was still itching to take my belt off and beat his bad ass, so it took me a second to finally put him on his feet after he nodded his understanding. Immediately, Vernique pulled him to her like I'd really hurt him or something, only pissing me off more. "Man, get his ass the fuck out my face!" I scoffed, waving her away as I pulled out my burner phone and powered it on. I didn't miss the look of hatred she sent my way before carrying Kash into the other room, but I'd handle her later. As soon as the screen lit up, I dialed the only number that I had saved in it and took a seat on the couch while it rang. It was obvious that I couldn't keep putting this shit off. I was gonna fuck around and kill my meal ticket and his mama if I kept dragging my feet, so I needed to get this drop done ASAP.

"Oh shit, you called right on time," Cash answered jovially, throwing me off for a second.

"You must got that money for me?"

"Naw, but I did run into yo' plastic, wig-wearing ass grandma though. We can do a fair trade right now, my son for the bitch that raised you, and I'll think about not comin' after yo' ass at a later date." The cockiness in his voice had my jaw clenching in anger.

"So you sayin' you don't got my money?" I asked for clarification, because out of everything else he'd said that was the only thing that I gave a fuck about.

"Did you just hear me, nigga? I'm bouta blow this old bitch's dentures out her mouth and you still askin' me about some money?"

"So, I don't like her evil ass! Put the bitch out her misery, but if you wanna see yo' son again you better get my money and meet me at Ridge Mall by the carousel at 8! If not, my grandma ain't gone be the only one gettin' put down! I'm done playin' with yo' ass!" I didn't give him a chance to respond before hanging up and throwing the phone across the room. It hit the wall with a crack and shattered into pieces. That shit only enraged me more. Leaving it there, I went in to take my frustrations out on Vernique. As soon as I opened the bedroom door and saw her with one foot out of the window, I ran over and grabbed her dumbass by her tracks.

"Urghhh, stupid ass bitch!"

"Run Kash! Go!" she screamed loudly, and I wasted no time punching her in the nose twice, instantly making her hands fly to her face as she hit the ground. I caught a glimpse of Kash disappearing around the bushes that lined the house. Cursing, I pulled my gun out, glad that I hadn't removed the silencer, and sent two bullets into her head. *Stupid ass bitch!* Once her body slumped to the floor, I tucked my gun back in my pants and raced outside, praying that his little ass hadn't gotten too far away. The block was completely empty since most of the people around there were at work this time of day. Looking both ways, I headed right, cursing Vernique for possibly fucking up my plans. I regretted not tying them both up from the beginning, but that would've been too much work having to untie them to eat or use the bathroom. That bitch had been so shook I didn't think I'd need to, and now I was kicking my own self in the ass because if Kash ran into the right person, it would have the police involved and that was some smoke I didn't need.

Hitting the corner, I slowed my pace down to a brisk walk at the sight of a small crowd. From where I was I could see about four people huddled in the middle of the sidewalk, and my heart pounded in my ears. My gut told me they had either seen Kash or were currently in possession of him, and when one of them pulled out their phone and began to pace, my suspicions were confirmed. Kash stood there crying while a lady sat crouched in front of him with a look of concern. Immediately, I halted in my steps and began to back pedal as he pointed down the street in my direction. Everyone's head turned my way at the same time, and I took off back toward the house.

Thankfully, none of them followed me, but I didn't know if that little nigga could identify my house or not. For sure the police would come knocking door to door and find out which crib he'd been in, then I'd have to answer for Vernique's dead ass along with kidnapping, and I wasn't trying to let that happen. As soon as I made it to the house, I grabbed as much as I could stuff into my gym bag, plus the bag of what I had left from Cash's trap. The fact that I'd only taken over the lease from a crackhead I knew gave me somewhat of a head start since the police would be looking for his ass instead of me until they figured it out, but by then I'd be long gone. I was mad enough to tear that bitch up and set it on fire, but I didn't have the time and a random ass fire would only lead the police there faster, so instead, I just finished grabbing my stuff and loaded up my car. With my funds running low, I didn't have very many places to go, but I planned to unload the rest of the drugs back in Milwaukee before leaving the Midwest all together. Wasn't no way Cash was going to let this shit slide and unless I got an army behind me, I was as good as dead.

By the time I climbed behind the wheel of my car, I could already hear an ambulance siren blaring. My paranoia at this point immediately told me they were there for Kash and that the police would be arriving soon. Busting a U-turn, I headed in the opposite direction of where I knew Kash was, punching the steering wheel in anger at how I'd let a pay day slip through my fingers.

CHAPTER FIVE
CASH

"Fuck!" Pissed, I sent my fist through the nearest wall, drawing all eyes to me. I'm sure the handful of niggas in the room thought I had lost my damn mind, and I felt like I for sure had. The nigga Lox just didn't know how bad his death was going to be once I finally caught up to his ass. Once again, he'd surprised the fuck out of me because I damn sure hadn't expected him to be so damn cold blooded. He didn't have any loyalty to anybody, and that meant I was wasting my time going after any of his people. Turning back to the old lady we had tied up, I crouched down into her face and she immediately cowered away. "I'm lettin' you go, understand? But if you *ever* mention this shit to anybody, I'm comin' back and puttin' a bullet in your head," I warned, and she nodded vigorously. The fear in her eyes was enough for me to believe she'd keep this shit to herself, but I still snatched the tape off her mouth.

"I promise, I won't say nothin', I swear!" I eyeballed her for a second longer before standing to my full height and motioning to my nigga Q.

"Come untie her so we can go." His face immediately balled up at that, and he looked between the two of us confused.

"Let her go! I thought—"

"I don't pay you to think, I pay you to do what the fuck I say, and I said let her go!" He snapped his mouth shut and gave me a stiff mug before bending to cut her loose.

"What I miss?" Dinero stepped into the dining room with his forehead bunched as he took in the sight before him. He'd taken his lovesick ass in the kitchen to try and call Ca'Mahri before I got on the phone with Lox.

"He lettin' her go," Q answered before I could, sounding disappointed.

"No shit, Sherlock. For what?"

"That nigga don't give a fuck about her, that's why. He basically told me to kill her ass." Scoffing, I watched as Q finally took the last of the ropes off. With her hands and feet free, she rubbed her wrists but remained in the chair, looking between all of us fearfully.

"And you don't think he was tryna use reverse psychology on you?" he cocked his head and asked, but I was already dismissing that idea.

"Naw, he was dead serious. He's all about the money and don't give a fuck about shit else, and I ain't tryna have no dead old lady on my conscience for nothin'," I huffed, locking eyes with her as I spoke. I didn't even need to see Dinero to know that he strongly disapproved. His paranoid ass was trying to be extra careful, but there was no need. Irritated, I whistled for my team, pointing toward the door with my thumb so they could head out. Once they were all gone, me and Dinero followed suit, except he stopped right next to her and leaned down into her ear.

"Forget you ever saw us," he told her, tapping the gun on his waist as he walked past her for emphasis. Shaking my head, I followed the other men out with him right on my heels. We needed to get our shit together and get back to Chicago since evidently, that's where he was. All the hell we'd been raising in the week we'd been there and the nigga hadn't come out of hiding nor called off this bullshit ass ransom. I hadn't spared any of his workers like I'd done his grandma, and I'd burned down every trap the nigga had set up so he didn't have shit to fall back on, but it was obvious he was going to ride the Kash train until the wheels fell off. The only good thing I could take from that shit was that he didn't have any backup, so if we caught him slipping at the mall, then this shit would be over.

"Now tell me what the fuck happened in there," Dinero demanded as soon as we were alone in the car and headed back to the hotel.

"Nothin' happened. I told that nigga I had his peoples and he encouraged me to kill the bitch. Then he turned around and insisted we do the drop *tonight* at Ridge Mall."

"Damn, his ass don't give a fuck about shit!" He shook his head in disbelief. "Did he give you a sign of life?"

The question had my heart dropping into my stomach. I hadn't even asked to hear my son's voice and I damn sure hadn't heard the sounds of a toddler in the background. I tried to reason with myself that Vernique was there and probably kept him quiet, at least I hoped that's what was happening. I'd been on go since he called me the first time and hadn't really considered her role in all of this. Whether by choice or by force, she'd brought that nigga to our son without regard for his life, and that was punishable by death. The difference between us was I'd gladly take a bullet to protect our son. Shit, I'd take the whole clip before I put him in danger. Clearly, Vernique wasn't concerned with his safety so I wasn't going to be concerned with hers. I was pretty sure that Lox wouldn't fuck up his money and hurt him, though, he wasn't stupid enough to do that.

"I didn't think to, but I know Kash is alive. Ain't no way he not," I insisted. I had to believe that or else my heart would fucking stop. Out of the corner of my eye, I could see Dinero nodding in agreement.

"Yeah, nephew good," was all he said before turning the radio up. We rode the rest of the way to the room in silence and after we packed up our few belongings, we were on the road and headed back to the city.

A few hours later I'd just finished filling two small duffels with money when my phone started going off in my pocket. It was creeping toward eight so I hurried to pull it out just in case it was Lox, but it was only my OG. Before I could slide the bar across the screen she'd hung up and immediately called right back.

"What's up, Ma? I'm kinda in the middle of some—"

"They found him! They found Kash, baby!" she cried, cutting me off, and my knees instantly got weak. I fell into the chair closest to me, unable to hear anything else she was saying. As strong as I was, I hadn't ever felt so weak, not even when Kash first got snatched. I wiped away the tears that were flooding down my face only for a fresh set to immediately trail them.

"Ma, please—" My voice cracked and I cleared my throat before continuing. "Please don't tell me my baby is...is—" I couldn't even bring myself to say the word.

"What? Cash, what are you talking about boy? Some woman found him running down Racine by himself and called the police! Kash is fine, they have him at the police station, me and your daddy on the way there now! I'm bouta send you the address, hurry yo' ass up!" she fussed, hanging up. With the phone still pressed to my ear, I released a sigh of relief and sent a silent thank you to the man upstairs for my son's safe return.

My phone chimed with the text from my mama, snapping me out of my moment of praise, and as soon as I confirmed it was the address, I was on my feet heading toward the door. A million thoughts were running through my head as I jumped in my truck and sped off.

I rode the entire way in silence except for the occasional phone call or alert, which I ignored. I didn't wanna talk to a soul until I saw my boy with my own two eyes. It was hard to believe he'd even gotten away, and I couldn't help but feel guilty for not being able to be the one to save him. The what ifs were killing me and the joy I'd been feeling was quickly being overshadowed by my self-deprecating thoughts. Without realizing it, I'd made it to the station, and instead of going to the visitor parking lot I haphazardly pulled into a spot right out front that was strictly for police vehicles. Shutting my truck off, I stepped out, daring any of the officers that were out there to say something to me. I hadn't made the connection when my OG had first called, but the captain and a couple of his bitch ass employees were on our payroll, and the fact that none of them had reached out to me directly had me heated. I guess they felt like my pops was the next best thing, but when it came to Kash Zyree Banks, there was no next best thing.

"Sir, I'm sorry, but you can't—hey, somebody stop him!"

The lady at the front desk was talking to me and trying to draw the officers' attention, but I continued on my path to the back of the station and busted into Captain Fields's office. He was on the phone when I entered but at the sight of me, he quickly hung up with wide eyes.

"Cash, man listen, it was a rookie and a straight that answered the call. I didn't even find out about this until right before you!" He was already pleading his case, but I wasn't trying to hear it.

"I look like I give a fuck about any of that shit?" I looked around his messy office before my eyes landed back on him. "You the boss of this muhfucka, right? And I pay you for inside information, which makes me yo' boss," I said slowly so his dumb ass could follow along.

"Yeah, but—"

"Ain't no buts. You dropped the fuckin' ball by lettin' them muhfuckas answer the call! Then I'm the last nigga to know when that shit trickled down the pipeline! This shit needs to stay private; no reporters, no news article, *no* fuckin' police report!"

"Come on, Cash, be realistic! There's no way I can do any of that without raising a few eyebrows around here!" he whined, and his beady blue eyes went to the door nervously. For him to have been so deep in the underworld, he was coming off too pussy for my liking and I had to resist the urge to go across his shit. It was a shame I had to walk a nigga through how to do their job, and I really didn't have time for that, so I elected to threaten him instead.

"You're gonna do it or you gon' be burying Savannah and those bitch ass sons of yours. Which one you think gon' be easier for you to handle?" I stared him right in the eyes so it was clear I wasn't bullshitting. After a few seconds, he clamped his mouth shut and gave me a stiff nod.

"I'll get right on that." Humble was the best way to describe his voice now as he conceded, but I would still be keeping an eye on his scary ass.

"You do that, but take me to my son first."

With his shoulders slumped in defeat, he came from around the desk mumbling, "Of course," and I followed him out into the hallway where it seemed like all eyes were on us. I commanded attention everywhere I went, it came with the Banks name, so it didn't faze me, but I could tell that shit had the captain even more nervous.

"What the fuck are y'all lookin' at! Get back to work!" he snapped, forcing all of them to put their attention back on whatever they were working on. I was sure he was frustrated and already thinking of a way to handle the task I'd given him, and as long as it got done I didn't give a fuck.

He led me down a long hall and ushered me into a conference room where I saw my OG, pops, Dinero, and Kash. My mama had him sitting on her lap, squeezing the life out of him while he watched a video on her phone, but as soon as he heard the door, he was wiggling down to get to me.

"Daaaadddddddy!" Just hearing his little voice was enough to bring me to my knees, and I realized it was because up until that point I wasn't sure I would see him again. There were plenty of times when a ransom attempt didn't go as planned and families were never reunited. I liked to think that some shit like that would never happen to us because of our name and status, but clearly, that wasn't true. No doubt there'd always be some thirsty ass bum out there willing to go to extreme measures for a bag, and the risk would only get worse as my kids got older and came into contact with more people. If I needed to, I'd have security following them around twenty-four-seven, though, just to keep myself from feeling the way I felt when Kash was gone.

My eyes stung as I scooped him up in my arms and hugged him tightly. His little boney arms squeezed my neck and like he'd only been visiting his mama and not in danger, he began to tell me about the time he'd been away. I let him enthusiastically fill me in on how mean his mama's boyfriend was, how he made them both cry, and how he only fed him hotdogs and noodles and never the good stuff. If the situation wasn't so serious I might have laughed at his description of what happened. I let him talk my ear off for a few minutes, before my pops cleared his throat and gave me a look. Even though I didn't want to let my mans out of my sight, I knew I had to get the actual details of what happened.

"Aye man, go sit with Granny for a minute while I step outside, ayite." Immediately, a look of disappointment crossed his face and I quickly reassured him. "It will only take a second then we can leave and get some McDonald's." The mention of the restaurant had a huge smile appearing on his face and he cheered before running back over to my mama.

"We'll be right back, baby." My pops was already moving toward the door as he spoke and instinctively, the captain followed with me and Dinero bringing up the rear. I pulled the door shut behind us and leaned up against the wall while Captain Fields huddled closer so our conversation wouldn't be overheard by the other officers milling about.

"So, where's the people who had my grandson, Cap?" Pops got straight to the point, and I could tell he was itching to get his hands on Lox just like I was.

"Uhhh, there was no sign of Lamont Thomas at the house that Kash said he was being held at, and Vernique Porter was found dead at the scene with multiple gunshot wounds to the head. From what Kash told us, she'd helped him out of the window and was supposed to come too but ended up yelling for him to run," Fields explained, and I locked eyes with Dinero. We'd been unsure of Vernique's role in this, but her helping Kash to get away and then being killed gave us a little more insight.

"We found out that he'd taken over the lease from a George Govan, a well-known drug addict, a couple months ago but other than that, they didn't know anything about him and he didn't leave anything at the apartment that we could use to locate him." I hated that once again that nigga had slipped through our fingers, but without money and with his leverage gone, it was only a matter of time before we caught up to him.

"Ayite, don't worry about it unless one of your boys catches up to him before I do," I grit just as two young looking white cops approached.

"Is this the family of Kash Banks?" one asked, trying to make his voice much deeper than it was. I could tell that he was still riding on a high after being the one to bring Kash home and discovering a murder victim.

"Uh yeah, but—"

"Good, I actually have some follow-up questions about what happened." The nigga cut the captain off and immediately pulled out his notepad. "How long had Kash been missing?"

"I'm gone have to stop you right there. I just got my son back and I'd like to take him to the hospital and get him checked out since y'all failed to do so. Now if you'll excuse me." I mugged him before brushing past to go back into the conference room to get Kash so I could get the fuck up out of there. The short amount of time I'd spent in the police station had been too long, and all I wanted to do was lay up under my baby mama and my son.

CHAPTER SIX
CA'MAHRI

"I'm ready, Jamal," I chimed, coming out of the bedroom with my bag on my shoulder. Finally, we were going to be leaving the penthouse and I couldn't be happier. Happy that they'd gotten Kash back safely and even happier that I could finally move freely. Being locked away in the luxury apartment besides for work or school had been giving me Rapunzel vibes and I didn't like that shit at all, especially considering my current attitude with Dinero. I'd fucked up and allowed my emotions to get the best of me after we'd left the hospital and he sweet talked me right out of my damn panties. Immediately after I came down from my orgasmic high, though, I came to my senses and remembered that I was supposed to be distancing myself, not growing more emotionally attached. That's why instead of waiting to bring up taking a break until after they got Kash back, I blurted it out during post coital conversation. The look of hurt that had flashed across Dinero's face was one I wouldn't forget, but it didn't change my mind, and that had his switch flipping from hurt to angry real quick. The argument that followed was draining to say the least, especially since I was trying to act unbothered. Truth be told, I was extremely confused, but if he knew I was unsure he would've surely used that to his advantage. That's why I was so glad that Cash encouraged him to leave, or else he'd have been getting his way like usual.

We hadn't talked since they'd been gone, only because I was refusing to answer his calls, but I knew the guard dogs he had on us kept him in the loop about everything going on in their absence, just like Camille's motormouth ass. She knew everything and instead of seeing my point of view, her suddenly hopeless romantic ass was on his side, which I really didn't like. It seemed like our roles had been reversed, with me being the skeptical one and her being the one that looked beyond flaws in the name of love. Still, regardless of her opinion, I used the opportunity of her meeting Cash at the hospital and having two of the guards to escort to my benefit. We were in the clear to finally leave, obviously, and I was going to make my departure while Dinero was at the hospital with his family. At least that had been the goal until I stepped into the living room and saw him instead of the guard, Jamal. He was sitting on the couch with his elbows resting on his knees as he looked out at nothing. The smile on my face instantly dropped and my spine straightened.

"You that done you was gon' sneak out while you thought I was occupied?" It came out as a question, but I knew him well enough to know it was an observation more than anything. My heart was pounding out of my chest, like I was a child getting caught trying to run away, and I struggled to find something to say in the tense moment.

"Where's Jamal?" I questioned lamely, irritated with myself that, that was all I could come up with. Chuckling, he brought his dark eyes my way.

"Really, Ca'Mahri? That's yo' fuckin' concern right now?

You somethin' else, man." He shook his head in disbelief before standing to his feet. For some reason I felt attacked, like he was minimizing my feelings and accusing me of some shit in a way, and I got heated.

"I'm somethin' else?" I scoffed, palming my chest. "You're the reason I have to go through these measures when all I was trying to do was take some time apart, figure out if being with you is something I can handle—"

"Fuck outta here with that shit, bruh! Now you can't handle being with a nigga? After one fuckin' night? You gotta come better than that!" He quickly moved across the floor and was standing in my face, looking down at me angrily.

"A night where my sister witnessed a murder and was attacked, at y'all supposedly safe place of residence! Knowing something could happen is one thing, but having something happen is completely different! My sister could've died that night because of her attachment to your family, so if I want to take some time apart then I feel like that's a reasonable request!" I shouted, poking myself in the chest. It was unbelievable to me that the same caring and understanding Dinero that had reeled me in was trying to force my hand instead of allowing me to do what I felt was best for me. I really thought I'd never see the day when there was so much of a disconnect between us. He was quiet, just staring at me with a bunch of different emotions burning in his eyes, so I attempted to explain in a softer way. "Look, I do love you, I just need to see if this is a life I can see myself living with you." I searched his eyes for understanding, but there was only that storm brewing behind them, before they just completely went blank. With a stiff nod, he took a step out of my space and my heart dropped at the immediate detachment.

"Well, this all yo' shit?" He motioned to my bag, snatching it up before I could even wrap my mind around the question.

"Uhhh, yeah," I mumbled to his back since he was already heading toward the door with it tossed over his shoulder. Unsure of what had happened, I followed him out and into the elevator where he silently pressed the button to take us to the main lobby. I didn't know what to think about his sudden change in demeanor, but it didn't stop me from trying to gauge his mood as we rode down. "How's Kash and Ms. Dorothea doing?"

The nasty look he gave me shut that shit right down, and I clamped my mouth shut for the rest of the ride. When the bell finally dinged announcing that we'd arrived at the lobby, he stepped off quickly like he couldn't stand to be in such close quarters. With long powerful strides, he was halfway to the building's front doors in seconds while I struggled to keep up. Thankfully, it was getting late so there wasn't much activity and no one but the doorman to witness how awkward we looked.

His truck was already sitting right outside running, and he wasted no time tossing my bag into the backseat before holding open the passenger door for me. That's when I saw Jamal come onto the sidewalk with an apologetic look on his face and realized that Dinero had called him down to babysit his car while he came up to retrieve me. After I climbed inside, they had a brief conversation and then Dinero hopped behind the wheel, pulling off at full speed. I was still trying to find the words to break the tension even though he'd cut his radio up to the max. It wasn't long, though, before he was cutting it back down, and my chest tightened wondering what he was about to say.

"Where you gettin' dropped off to?" he asked flatly without ever taking his eyes off the road, and I instantly felt my attitude creeping back up.

"It's no reason for you to be all dry, Dinero. I told you—"

"Is you goin' to Camille's or your parents', before I miss my exit?" He finally looked my way and I almost wished he hadn't. This was a side of him I hadn't experienced in a long ass time, and I wasn't sure how to take it. On one hand, his coldness would make the separation a little easier but on the other, I was salty that he was so quick to completely wash his hands of me.

Stammering, I said the first thing that popped into my head, just wanting to be out of his presence. "Uh, just take me to Camille's," I answered weakly, and he turned the radio up before I even got her name out of my mouth fully. With the precision of a race car driver, he crossed the three lanes and got off on the first exit. The way he was speeding had us pulling up to my sister's apartment in less than the half hour it would've normally taken. I opened my mouth to speak but he was already coming around the back of the truck, first grabbing my bag and then pulling open my door. As mean as he was being, his chivalry surprised me, but I took his outstretched hand anyway, stepping out on the curb. I reached for my bag, figuring this was it, but he hit me with a serious mean mug and kept it just out of reach.

"Stop fuckin' playin' with me, shorty. You might've switched up, but I'm still me," he spat, walking off toward the apartment. Even though I didn't appreciate his insult, I kept my displeasure to myself and once we made it to the porch, I reached into my bag for the keys and let myself in.

"Well, thank y—" I'd barely crossed the threshold and had the words out before he'd dropped my bag inside and walked back down the sidewalk, leaving me feeling salty enough to kick my bag aside and slam the door.

"Soooo, y'all really done fuckin' around? Like done, done?" Nova asked with her nose crinkled doubtfully before taking a sip of her drink. It had been a couple of weeks since Dinero had dropped me off at Camille's and I was still feeling the sting of our last encounter. Of course, I hadn't heard from him and I was fighting the urge to call, because I missed him so much. I'd been so stressed about the way things ended that I hadn't even had time to think over the things I was supposed to be thinking over. Camille helped put my mind slightly at ease with her mini updates on him and Ms. Dorothea, but it wasn't the same. At the same time, though, it hurt knowing that there wasn't shit wrong with his ass, but I could accept that I'd brought it on myself moving off of hasty emotions. Shrugging, I finished chewing the chicken salad sandwich I'd bought before saying.

"I guess so. He's still not talking to me and it's been weeks."

"Well, have you tried to call him?" she countered, and I couldn't help but roll my eyes.

"Hell naw, with her scary ass," Camille popped up, answering before I could as she pulled up a chair. Her face had healed nicely and she'd returned to work a week before, much to Cash's dismay. Even I had been a little worried about her returning to life as usual after such a traumatic experience, but obviously, my concern was unwarranted seeing as how normal she seemed. She immediately started digging into her lasagna like she hadn't just insulted me, and I waved her irritating ass off.

"I'm not sca—"

"Quit lyin', hoe. You're scared shitless." She sucked her teeth, cutting me off. "I told you not to do that shit, but yo' ass just wouldn't listen." This wasn't the first time I'd gotten an I told you so from her since I'd asked for the break from Dinero, and just like every other time, we got into a damn debate with Nova's eyes bouncing between each of us.

"Okay, but it's not like I was expecting this to be something permanent. I only wanted some time to figure some shit out," I hissed lowly so the other people on their lunch breaks wouldn't be in my business, and she twisted her lips up at me.

"And you wanted him to what, be okay with it? Regardless of what happened, Dinero ain't been nothing but good to you. Way better than any other nigga, and I ain't just sayin' that 'cause he's my boo's brother."

"I mean, damn girl, what did you expect though? Didn't you say like two bitches broke up with him for the same shit before?" Nova chimed in with a frown, and Camille once again added her two cents.

"Exactly! His ass probably got PTSD and all types of emotional baggage from that shit and she basically did the same damn thing. Even if it was only supposed to be a small break, how was he supposed to know that?"

Huffing because I didn't have a good rebuttal for either of their points and I felt like they were ganging up on me, I crossed my arms underneath my breasts. It was true, Dinero had shared with me about the two serious relationships he'd had that ended badly in the past, but I didn't feel like our situation was anything like that. The thought of our little separation hadn't seemed permanent when I played it out in my head. I knew with him being the type of man that liked to be in control at all times he'd be kind of mad, and maybe even refuse, but I damn sure hadn't expected him to completely shit on me the way he did.

"He was supposed to know because I told him. He didn't even hear me out, though, he immediately shut down on me. If you would've seen the way he was acting then you'd understand why I haven't called!" I fumed, grabbing my tray and getting up to toss it since my appetite was suddenly gone due to the nervous twisting in my stomach.

"'Cause you know yo' scary ass was wrong, that's why!" Camille's petty ass called out behind me, and both them bitches started cackling wildly. Her words followed me out of the cafeteria, and I pulled my phone out of my scrubs seeing that I still had about fifteen minutes left of my break, so I decided to prove my sister and Nova wrong. Going to Dinero's contact, I quickly clicked it before I could change my mind. I held my breath, heart pounding as it rang in my ear until the call was picked up. Immediately, I could hear a woman giggling before Dinero's voice could be heard.

"Yo' T, you better stop playin' and eat that expensive ass shit I just bought before this shit turn Dutch!" he quipped and, I hung up with my jaw dropped in shock. Hurt wasn't even the word to describe my feelings after hearing that shit. I felt played but more than anything, I was pissed off that his ass had rushed right into hype ass Tania's arms after swearing things weren't like that. I still had a few hours left in my shift, so there wasn't anything I could do about it right then, but Dinero Banks was going to have to see me before it was all said and done!

CHAPTER SEVEN
DINERO

I t seemed like things had somewhat returned to normal since Kash had been found, and that meant we could get back to business. The nigga Lox was on the run so he wasn't a serious threat, but he would still be held accountable for what he'd done when we did finally catch up to him. Although Kash wasn't aware of how serious the situation was, he'd still been violated and had lost his mother in the process. He really didn't grasp the concept that Vernique wasn't coming back because for the first few days, he kept asking why the police didn't get her too. After a while, he seemed to accept that she wasn't coming and since he'd grown used to not seeing her as often, he just stopped asking. Between me, Cash, and our parents, we tried to keep him busy enough that he didn't feel any type of emptiness, and it seemed to be working.

We also were still trying to deal with my granny being hospitalized. She was still in a coma but the doctors were recording positive brain activity and believed she could be waking up at any point. We rotated sitting by her side so when she did wake up it'd hopefully be to a family member's face and not some random doctor or nurse.

I was being stretched thin as fuck between the business, monitoring my granny, kicking it with Kash, and spending time with Tania. As fucked up as it may have seemed, the shit was helping me to keep my mind off Ca'Mahri. Once again, the drug game had taken a woman out of my life and just like the other times, it put me in a fucked-up headspace, but I had so much other shit going on I didn't have time to mope. Money needed to be made and my family needed me to be there for them, so I had to push my hurt feelings to the backburner. That shit was much easier said than done.

My phone rang, snatching me out of my thoughts, and seeing that it was Tania brought a smirk to my face. Shorty had been doing good in her program and was looking just like her old self again. After being part of the reason she was even in the situation to begin with, it felt good to see her getting back on track.

"Hey, what's up T?"

"Hey Dinero," she cooed, and I could tell she had a big ass grin on her face. "How are you? How's the family?"

"Shiiiit, we're all good, just waiting on Dorothea's ass to wake up and shit," I told her, shrugging my shoulders like she could see me. "How you doin'? Don't yo' ass got group comin' up soon?"

"Dang, let me find out you know my schedule." She giggled, and I didn't miss the flirtation in her tone. Truth be told, the more time I spent with her the more I noticed her giving me that look. I wasn't out to have her falling back in love or nothing, but it was obvious that's where things were headed, and I knew I'd have to let her down easy at some point.

"You the one that told me what they be having y'all asses

doing every day, don't be tryna make me sound like a damn stalker!"

"I mean, it is stalkerish behavior to memorize it, but I'ma let you make it though," she said playfully, and we shared a laugh. "Anyway, I was actually just calling because we have a family day coming up and I wanted to know if you'd come since I don't fuck with my actual family." Her voice had suddenly turned nervous like she was worried about my response, even though there was no need. She should've known by now how much I fucked with her, and if kicking it around a bunch of addicts and their dysfunctional ass families for a day was what she needed, then it was done.

"Yeah, I can do that, just tell me when and I'll be there." She was already squealing in my ear before I got my answer all the way out, only making my grin widen at making her happy.

"Oh gosh, thanks so much! I didn't want to be the only person who didn't have anybody show up. But I'll give you the details soon, I gotta go get ready for group."

"Don't thank me for that lil' shit, you know I got you," I said truthfully. Since she didn't have anyone, I felt responsible for her and I'd make sure she was good even when she got out, which wasn't going to be much longer. We ended up talking a few minutes more before ending the call.

"Fuck you in here grinnin' about lookin' like the Joker and shit?" Cash cracked, stepping into my office with two bags from Chick-fil-A. He tossed me one and then dropped down into one of the empty chairs in front of my desk.

"Shut up, bitch! Ain't nobody grinnin'," I quickly denied and focused on my food, hoping that he'd change the subject, but, of course, he didn't.

"Ohh, I'ma bitch now 'cause I caught yo' ass in here with heart eyes! Let me find out you wasn't thinkin' 'bout sis and I'm tellin'."

We hadn't talked too much about what had happened between me and Ca'Mahri besides the basics, which was that she wanted a break after all the shit that had gone down. In his mind we were still getting back together at some point, but I wasn't fucking with shorty. She'd basically dropped me when I was going through some shit and all over a situation that didn't even directly involve her. Even after I sent her off from the hospital I was willing to fight for her, but once I got to the penthouse and she brought that shit back up, knowing I was preparing to go out in the field. Our days apart hadn't even done anything because as soon as I got back, she was just ready to dip out on a nigga.

I shook my head just thinking about the way Ca'Mahri had shitted on me, and my mood instantly soured.

"I'm a grown ass man, ain't no tellin' on me, nigga. Besides, she's the one that wanted a break, so that's what I'm givin' her." I shrugged, stuffing my mouth with waffle fries, and he frowned like I'd said the dumbest shit in the world.

"See, that's yo' muhfuckin' problem now! Let Camille try to pull that shit with me and I'm lockin' her pregnant ass up! Fuck around and put some cuffs on her ass! She already know not to play with me." Just the look on his face let me know he was dead ass serious, and I couldn't do shit but shake my head at his slow ass.

"Yo' ass crazy, boy! If I gotta do all that just to keep her, then I don't need her," I said adamantly.

"And that's why you lost yo' girl, man. These new females is different, they love that crazy shit! They don't want that old sweet RnB shit you on, these City Girls and Hotties out here!"

"Man, get yo' ass out my office, bro."

"You know what, fuck you! I ain't never givin' yo' lonely ass no more advice!" he talked shit as he stood and gathered his trash from my desk.

"I'd rather be lonely than holding females hostage to make them stay!" I shot back as he made his way to the door. Instead of saying anything back, he raised his middle finger up at me as he exited. His ass could say whatever he wanted, I wasn't forcing no bitch to be with me, not even Ca'Mahri.

———

It was the day of Tania's family event and I was surprised at how many families had actually ended up coming. As I maneuvered through the thick crowd of guests in search of Tania, I was stopped a handful of times by different women trying to shoot their shot, from guests to patients. I finally spotted her off to the side with her counselor and instantly breathed a sigh of relief. As if she felt my presence, her eyes found mine and we both smiled as I closed the short distance between us.

"I'm so glad you made it!" she gushed, jumping into my arms, and I embraced her tightly, noting how much more weight she'd gained.

"I told you I would, you know I always keep my promises," I told her, pulling back just enough to take her in. I had to admit she was looking good as fuck with her long hair pressed and hanging down past her shoulders with a simple middle part. The makeup she had on was minimal and her nude dress fit her perfectly, giving me a good view of her shapely figure. She looked good as fuck and I couldn't keep my eyes off of her.

Beaming, she nodded and batted her eyelashes. "I know," she simpered, eyeing me like she wanted to take a bite. With an uncomfortable chuckle, I turned to the counselor and extended my hand for a shake, not liking the knowing look on her face.

"Hello, it's nice to see you again."

"Likewise." Her voice dropped and she glanced between

the two of us before excusing herself. "I'll leave you two to it. I have rounds to make."

After she walked off, we stood talking for a few minutes and she introduced me to some of the people in the program with her before grabbing me some food. I had eaten before I'd gotten there so I wasn't hungry, but I still accepted the burger and fries.

"Hey, I wanna show you something." We'd been done eating for about ten minutes when she grabbed my hand and pulled me away before I could object. She took me down the hall where their rooms were, which I was sure wasn't allowed, and opened the last door on the left, waving me inside. Her room was set up dorm style, with a twin bed on one side and a desk on the other, and I could tell all the other ones were the exact same. I took in the pictures on the walls and stopped next to where she had some accomplishment ribbons. I was still reading them when she came up behind me, pressing her chest into my back and sliding her hands around me.

"Aye, aye, what you on?" I questioned, removing her hands and turning to face her.

"Nothing." She shrugged with a smirk. "I can't hug you now?"

"Fa' sho, I just wasn't expecting that shit." It was a lie. Her ass was making me uncomfortable as hell, but I wasn't trying to disappoint her on her special day. She was already inching toward me trying to look seductive, and I stepped back, getting trapped between her and the wall.

"I'm just trying to look out for you the way you look out for me," she damn near whispered, wrapping her arms around my neck and pressing her lips to mine. After a few seconds, I realized what I was doing, though, and pried her off me.

"Aye, you trippin' T! I fuck with you, but shit ain't like that with us no more!" Just like I knew it would, hurt flashed across her face before she broke into tears. I watched in disbelief as she childishly ran to her bed and buried her face in her pillow. As confused as I was by her reaction, I wasn't trying to stay and make shit worse. Instead, I made my exit, hoping that we could sweep this shit under the rug in a couple of days.

CHAPTER EIGHT
CAMILLE

I'd been putting off going to see Ms. Dorothea because I couldn't stand the sight of her hooked up to all types of machines, but I woke up that morning with a deep need to spend time with her. After handling my hygiene, I got dressed comfortably in a pair of black biker shorts, a gray graphic tee, and my black Steve Madden Maxima sneakers. I pulled my freshly washed and blow-dried hair into a high bun and swooped my baby hairs. By the time I was done getting dressed, Cash was up and moving around. He'd been coming to stay with me since I wasn't comfortable sleeping at his house.

Brushing past me, he pressed a kiss against the back of my neck. "Good morning, bae. What you got planned?" he asked as he stood over the toilet peeing.

"Not you using the bathroom in front of me," I huffed, unable to take my eyes off his dick as visions of the night before flashed through my mind.

"Not you starin' at my dick, with yo' freaky ass." He smirked cockily, finishing up and stuffing himself back into his shorts.

"Boy, boom! Wasn't nobody starin' at nothin'!" The lie rolled off my tongue as he came to stand next to me at the sink to wash his hands before grabbing his toothbrush.

"Lyin' ass."

Snickering, I continued to primp in the mirror, unable to stop myself from ogling him while he brushed his teeth. It was a shame how fine my baby daddy was, like I legit didn't know anybody who looked sexy while brushing their teeth, but Cash did. Really, he looked good doing anything and I found myself obsessed with him.

When he was done, he pulled me into his arms, giving me a couple of wet kisses and making me melt. The kiss deepened and he lifted me onto the sink with ease, pulling at my waistband, and I quickly stopped him.

"Aht, aht! I got somewhere to be." I shook him off, ignoring the agitated look on his face as I slid down.

"Fuck you goin'?" he asked like he was finally seeing that I was dressed for the first time. Resting my arms on his broad shoulders, I couldn't help but simper at his jealousy.

"I'm just bouta go visit with Ms. Dorothea, nigga, calm down." I rolled my eyes playfully and the tension left his shoulders.

"Oh ayite." He nodded, pecking my lips again. "I gotta go check on the apartments and then grab Kash from my mama. You wanna kick it with us later?"

"It depends on what we eatin'."

"Ha, I already know what I'ma be eatin'." He smirked devilishly before devouring my mouth again.

"Ahem! Can y'all save the freaky shit for the bedroom please!" Ca'Mahri appeared in the doorway with her face twisted and I chuckled, moving out of Cash's grasp.

"I hate to break it to you, sis, but we done been all over this muhfucka being nasty!"

"Cash!" I instantly shoved him, but he barely moved an inch, only grinning wider from our reactions.

"Ugh! I literally could've went my whole life without knowin' that!" she huffed, storming past us and ushering us out of the bathroom. Cash still thought it was hilarious as we made our way back into my bedroom.

"You ain't right for that."

"Her ass gon' be ayite." He shrugged, unbothered, stepping into his Nike slides. "I'm bouta go to the crib and get dressed. I'll see you later, right?" The mention of his house had my chest tightening, but I played it off with a nod and after giving me a quick kiss, he was gone. I honestly didn't know how he was able to go back there like someone hadn't been killed on the property. Despite the ease in which I'd gotten back to my life after Kash's kidnapping, I still couldn't bring myself to step foot back in his house and I didn't think I ever would. I already knew by the time the baby came we'd have issues when it came to our living arrangements, but I would cross that bridge when I got to it.

Almost two hours later, I was hesitantly entering Ms. Dorothea's room where a nurse was doing something with her IV. Upon seeing me, she smiled brightly. "Well, hello there!" she greeted, removing her gloves.

"Um, hi."

"It seems Ms. Dorothea doesn't ever have a shortage of visitors. Her son just left not too long ago. Come closer, don't be shy. I'm Alicia." She waved me over, noticing how I had yet to move away from the door. Forcing a smile, I took baby steps toward her bed. I really didn't know what I was expecting but besides the IV and the bandage on her head, she looked to just be sleeping. Her silver hair was spread neatly on her pillow and her hands were folded comfortably across her stomach.

"She looks so peaceful...like she's sleep," I spoke in a low tone, almost like I was speaking to myself.

"Yeah, I can tell she's a sweet lady with just the right amount of spice." Alicia described her perfectly without ever having witnessed her in action, and I nodded with a smile.

"That's exactly what she's like, and will read you in a minute," I added, placing my hand on top of hers.

"I can only imagine, but I have faith that she'll be getting up soon ready to give us all a piece of her mind." She gave me a light pat on the back and left the room, letting me know that if I needed anything to push the call button. Once she was gone, I pulled up a chair and got comfortable.

"I miss you, Dorothea girl. I'm sure everybody's probably already filled you in, but a lot's happened since you been in here gettin' your beauty rest. I know you said you were ready for a break from your bad ass grandsons, but this is not it!" I laughed as tears blurred my vision. I couldn't imagine her not ever waking up and being able to meet her great-grandbaby. Our last conversation replayed in my mind and despite the short amount of time she'd known me, I loved how quickly she took to me. I could imagine her now, snapping on me to stop crying before I stressed her baby out, and I quickly wiped my eyes. Ms. Dorothea gave some of the best advice and was always so warm, I just knew she had to be a big part of my pregnancy along with our parents.

I spoke with her for a little bit longer before eventually cutting on *Judge Mathis*. I barely listened as he called people crackheads and thieves while I scrolled on social media, and at some point I must have fallen asleep. A light tapping on my arm had me stirring, but I swatted it away. Pregnancy had my ass more tired than normal and even if I got a full eight hours of sleep I still needed a couple of naps throughout the day, and I didn't like people interrupting them. Coming out of my sleep-induced state, I could hear Judge Mathis's voice vaguely, but that wasn't the voice that had my eyes popping open.

"Girl, yo' ass in here snoring loud enough to wake the damn dead!" Sitting up, I locked eyes with Ms. Dorothea.

"Oh my god, you're up!" Jumping to my feet, I pressed the call light and then stepped out into the hall just in case I could get someone there faster. "She's awake! I need a doctor!"

"I wish you'd stop screaming," she fussed once I reentered the room with Alicia and a doctor in tow. I stood back and let them check her out even though I wanted to go over and squeeze her. To keep myself busy I called Cash and Ms. Keisha to let them know she had woken up. After they let me know they were on the way, I continued watching as the nurse checked her vitals and the doctor shined his little light in her face. The whole time they looked her over she was complaining and sounding just like her usual self. I couldn't do nothing but thank God for bringing her back to us.

After everybody had arrived with flowers and gifts, we ended up spending hours in her room while she cracked jokes and snapped on everybody for different reasons. Her waking up was just another heavy weight lifted off our shoulders and I could literally feel the change in the atmosphere. By the time visiting hours were over none of us wanted to leave, but Mr. Kendrick assured us he'd stay with her overnight. Of course, she fussed him out for hovering but I could tell she was happy to have her baby boy up under her no matter what she said.

"What you thinkin' 'bout?" Cash's voice broke through my thoughts. We were on our way back to my apartment with a sleeping Kash in the backseat snoring like he worked a job.

"Just how crazy today was." I couldn't keep the smile off my face as I looked at him. Even he had to shake his head with a smirk.

"Hell yeah, that shit's crazy. Who would've thought that all we had to do was send yo' snorin' ass up there to get my granny up!" he chortled, and I snatched my hand out of his so I could hit his shoulder.

"Boy, fuck you!" My fake attitude was given away by my laughter. He quickly grabbed my hand back into his and kissed the back of it.

"You know I'm just fuckin' with you, baby. On some real shit, though, you just keep giving my ass reasons to marry yo' fine ass. I ain't ever think I wanted what my parents have until I met you, and now I can't see myself livin' a life without you in it. This ain't no proposal neither so don't even look at me like that. I'm hood, but I ain't goofy enough to propose without a ring. I'm just lettin' you know that's where we headed."

Despite his disclaimer, I was unable to stop myself from crying after hearing the most romantic thing that he'd probably ever said. If it wasn't for Kash being in the car with us, I would've had his dick in my mouth. I couldn't believe I'd almost missed out by trying to make him a sneaky link, but I was so glad he didn't let that happen.

CHAPTER NINE

CASH

I'd been keeping my eyes and ears peeled for any type of news related to Kash's kidnapping in the media and was pleased that so far nothing had come up. I didn't know what Captain Fields had told his officers to keep their mouths shut, but I was glad it worked because I wasn't trying to kill them niggas. There was enough on my plate still looking for Lox and planning his murder, I didn't need any other distractions.

Adding another stack to the money counter, I nodded when it came out to be the right amount. Since I'd opened business back up, things had been running smoothly and that's what I liked to see. Having found Kash when we did, there wasn't much money that we'd missed out on, but we still needed to get Tino his shit, so niggas were hustling nonstop.

"Nigga, fuck is you quiet as fuck over there, ain't you?" I questioned my brother, breaking the silence that we'd been working in for the last half hour. His ass looked like he was in deep thought with his forehead all bunched and shit. "Aye! Dinero!" I said louder, tapping the table since he kept working like he hadn't heard me. His head shot up and I looked at him quizzically.

"Oh, what's up?"

"What's up? What got yo' head gone to the point you zoned out like that?" I wrapped a stack of money with a rubber band and set it aside with my eyes still focused on him as he shrugged and shook his head.

"I'm good, just tryna make sure this count right," he lied, wrapping his own stack before putting another one in the money counter. I was just about to let it slide because if he didn't want to talk about it I wasn't gone force him, but when his phone vibrated against the table, I peeped his body tense up at the name on the screen.

"See, I was gone let you make it, but what the fuck was that? Since when you out here ignoring T calls and shit?" I didn't want to assume shit when it came to my brother and his cracked-out ex, but that shit was weird as hell after he'd done so much to help her already. I dropped the money I was holding and gave him my undivided attention while he kept working, avoiding my glare.

"Tania kissed me, man," he finally said, sighing after, like just saying it aloud had taken a lot out of him. Being the petty nigga I was, I bucked my eyes and let my jaw drop.

"Nigga whaaaat! When this shit happen?"

"At her family day like a week ago—"

"I told yo' ass! Didn't I tell you her ass was gon' read too much into yo' *help*? Did you kiss her ass back? I know you ain't fuck, tell me you ain't do no grimy shit like that?" His face twisted up and he shot me a murderous look across the table.

"Nigga, fuck I look like! The kiss lasted a lil' longer than it should've 'cause she caught me off guard, but I stopped her and then left! I wouldn't do no shit like that!" he snapped, and my brow instantly went up.

"It's giving, yo' ass thought about it vibes though, bro." Even though his ass was in a dilemma, he immediately burst into laughter.

"Yo, I know you ain't just say that shit!"

"Aye man, fuck you, ayite! I been spendin' too much time around Camille's ass, but you know what the fuck I mean! Don't be tryna change the subject!" This hadn't been the first time I'd been looked at funny for using Camille's lingo, but I was usually able to catch myself. I was gone have to start tuning her ass out before that shit became a part of my everyday vernacular. When his ass finally got control of himself, he shrugged and looked off to the side.

"I mean, yeah, I thought about it, but that's as far as that shit went. I fuck with shorty and all, just not on that level. This is just about me helping her out. All I want is for her to get on her feet. I ain't do none of this to try and rekindle shit. Now her damn feelings hurt and I don't know how to be around her ass without it being awkward."

"Damn, that shit tough, bro, but I wouldn't beat myself up over it. Even though I told yo' ass this shit was gone blow up in yo' face, I was hopin' it wouldn't go this way," I admitted. I'd definitely felt like she was going to read more into the situation with as much attention as he was giving her. Tania's condition was delicate and there was a chance this whole thing could make her ass backslide, which would have them both fucked up in the end. "I wouldn't ignore her tho', you gone fuck around and make her relapse then you really gone feel shitty."

He nodded without speaking and answered his phone that was once again vibrating. I was thinking it was Tania again, but the way his demeanor changed, I knew that wasn't the case. "What! And y'all can't handle that?" he huffed angrily and paused to listen to whatever was being said before finally sighing. "Fine man, I'm on my way."

"What's goin' on?" I sat back watching as he stood up and began gathering his shit.

"Nothin', just some hype causing issues at one of the houses," he mumbled absentmindedly and continued to prepare to leave.

"Hold up, I might as well ride with." We'd already damn near finished the count besides a couple stacks, and I hurriedly put them in the counter before wrapping and bagging them too. Within ten minutes we were in his car and headed to the trap. I lit a blunt on the way and we passed it back and forth until we were pulling up to see a couple niggas standing on the porch. As soon as they saw us they straightened up like they'd been busy the whole time, and I shared a look with Dinero before climbing out.

"Sup Cash, sup D," they both rushed to speak as we walked up the cement steps. Still puffing my blunt, I moved past them with a head nod while my brother got on their asses about being lazy.

"Where dude at? It look quiet as hell over here to me," I noted, taking in how serene it was out there. The way Dinero had made it seem was like a nigga was causing a whole scene and disrupting the peace.

"Uhh, he out back," the tallest of the two said after they looked at each other, and I instantly felt my face forming into a frown.

"Fuck you mean he out back? Somebody back there holding that nigga hostage? I know y'all ain't kill his ass and put him in the back!" Dinero took the words right out of my mouth and their eyes ballooned as they rushed to deny it.

"Nah man!"

"Hell nah! I knocked his ass out and put him in the backyard! He thought we served pills here and I tried to tell him he was at the wrong house, but he started goin' off and drawing attention. I ain't know how long y'all was gone be so I put him to sleep so wouldn't nobody call the police or some shit!" Once again, it was the tall one speaking and even though he'd handled things, I still wanted to slap his ass for putting a passed-out hype in the backyard.

"We look like we go around pickin' up and droppin' off crackheads! Fuck you want us to do?" I didn't hide my displeasure as I glared between the two in irritation. They just shuffled around, avoiding my eyes, before Dinero finally tapped my arm.

"We already here, bro, let's just drop his ass off around the corner or some shit before he wake up drawing attention." I was surprised as fuck that he was even condoning this goofy shit, but I was just ready to get the fuck away from there.

"Ayite, but his ass riding in the trunk. He ain't coming to and fucking me up when he realize he been kidnapped!" I was already on my way off the porch as I spoke, but I stopped on the last step and turned to the one responsible. "And bring yo' ass 'cause you pickin' this nigga up!" He looked like he wanted to argue but ended up coming down off the porch and led the way while Dinero went to the car.

It was just starting to get dark so we were still able to see just not as much as if there were lights. By the time we made it to the back and near the broken down garage, Dinero was pulling up on the other side. In the corner, I could see a dark figure propped up on the gate and before I could get a good look, he was lifted up by dude's tall ass and thrown across his shoulders. Copying his steps so I wouldn't step in some shit to ruin my J's, we made it to the alley where Dinero was waiting with the trunk already open. I could hear the man beginning to moan, meaning that he'd be waking up soon, and I prepared myself to crack his ass if he did. What I wasn't expecting when I caught a glimpse of his face underneath the streetlights was for him to be familiar. I literally had to do a double take when he landed face up in the trunk, and I realized the hype that had been cutting up was Camille and Ca'Mahri's pops.

"What the fuck? Is that...?" Dinero caught on as soon as I did and looked down in his trunk confused.

"Hell yeah," I answered his unspoken question with a nod. Shock had us just staring at that nigga while I tried to think about if I'd seen any signs when I met him, but nothing came to mind. "Fuck man, get his ass outta there." Sighing, I stepped back to give him space, but he huffed like a bitch.

"Huh, I just put him in there!"

"I look like I give a fuck? Get my future father-in-law outta there!" His ass was already getting on my nerves and I ain't even know his name. My outburst had him rushing to do what I'd said, and I ran to open the back door up for him to put him in. Of course, his goofy ass hit his head on the roof, but I sent an evil glare his way that had him backing up as soon as the man was seated. Low key, I couldn't really blame him considering that Camille's daddy was a fairly big nigga and I knew that shit wasn't easy. Still, I wasn't going to tell him that. Slamming the door shut, I climbed in on the other side while Dinero put the car in gear and pulled off.

CHAPTER TEN
CA'MAHRI

As mad as I was at Dinero, I wasn't going to let that keep me from visiting Ms. Dorothea after finding out that she was awake. Since it was my day off, I decided to pick up some flowers and go see her. I knew there was a chance I'd run into Dinero, but I was hoping he'd be busy doing something else so I wouldn't. As mature as I was, I wasn't sure what I'd do if I was face to face with him again, so even as I shopped for a cute bouquet of roses, I prayed that I wouldn't run across him.

By the time I ducked into her room it was a little after eleven and she was sitting up in bed with her table across her. The nurse had just lifted the lid off her plate, and from where I stood I could make out the meatloaf, mashed potatoes, and peas she was being served. Just from the look on her face I could tell she didn't want it, and she immediately confirmed that assumption once the nurse left.

"I don't know who they think is eatin' this shit, but it ain't gone be me!" she grumbled, pushing the table from over her with her nose scrunched up. "Come on over here, girl, I know you ain't gone stand at the door the whole time."

"Hey, Ms. Dorothea." I chuckled, inching closer. She was clearly her regular old self and it was a breath of fresh air.

"Hey baby, those flowers for me?" she questioned, taking in the bouquet as I set it down on her nightstand.

"Yes ma'am—"

"You should've brought me somethin' to eat. I got plenty nuff flowers, but thank you, I guess," her ass snapped, and I couldn't help thinking that she was the true definition of a sour patch kid, just like Cash. "Why I'm just now seeing you up here?" She looked up at me expectantly and I fumbled to find a reason. I doubted that anyone had told her about the breakup with her just coming out of a coma, and I damn sure didn't want to be the one to break the news to her.

"Work and school is crazy right now. This is my first day off from both since you woke up," I lied and let my eyes roam around the room, unable to meet her scrutiny.

"Mmhmm, you sure it ain't got nothin' to do with whatever goin' on between you and Dinero?" I froze and looked back at her, shocked.

"We don't—"

"Aht, don't lie. I might be old but I ain't no damn fool! I can tell when some shit is goin' on, it's just a matter of what's goin' on. Now hand me that fruit cup since that's 'bout the only edible thing on that tray." I instantly did what she'd said, pulling off the plastic film and tucking the spoon in it before handing it to her. She took a couple bites and then pointed to the chair next to her bed. "Go ahead and tell me what done happened with y'all."

The last thing I wanted was to go over everything that had happened between me and her grandson, mostly because she may take the same stance that Ms. Keisha had. Trying to explain to his damn grandmother that I'd asked him for a break, and during that time he'd been spending time with his ex was uncomfortable to think about let alone to say out loud. Taking a seat, I nervously played with my fingers and tried to find the right words.

"Umm, some things happened after you came to the hospital, that I wasn't comfortable with, so I felt like maybe I should take some time to myself. Dinero agreed but days turned into weeks and we just never got back on track." I shrugged, suddenly feeling emotional. I blinked back tears, not wanting to show how bad this had affected me. Not telling her about the shit with Tania seemed like I was letting him off the hook, but our breakdown had happened before that and I wasn't trying to badmouth him at the moment.

"Well, first of all, you should never feel bad for putting yo' self first. A lot of women end up bitter and going through hell because they allowed other people to force them into situations they didn't wanna be in. Shit, I know a few of 'em. With that being said, it takes a certain type of woman to handle the life the Banks men live. Every woman Dinero has tried to love wasn't ever the one, and regardless of what you think, I know it's because you are." She nodded to emphasize her point. "Mark my words, y'all gone end up together."

"But what if we can't get it right?" My voice cracked and I lost the battle with my tears, unable to stop a few from spilling out onto my cheeks, but I quickly swiped them away.

"Well, I wouldn't worry about that, baby, Granny is always right. You better ask about me." She winked and we shared a laugh before moving on to lighter conversation while she finished her fruit cup. Before I knew it an hour had passed and I was enjoying myself, as Ms. Dorothea talked shit about everything from the hospital food to the aides. She literally had me cracking up, only for my laughter to get caught in my throat when the door swung open and Dinero stepped inside.

Immediately, it felt like every bit of air left the room, filling up with his cologne instead, and my heart began to beat uncontrollably. He looked good, better than good. His hair was freshly cut and his beard neatly lined up like he'd just got out of his barber's chair, even though I knew that wasn't the case since he was wearing a suit. He'd taken his jacket off and only had on the vest, which was somehow even sexier to me. *Fine ass bastard!*

Rolling my eyes, I turned back to Ms. Dorothea to find her wearing a knowing look. Something told me that she knew he was going to be coming up there, and when he came over to the other side of her bed and placed a Panera Bread bag in her lap, that thought was confirmed.

"I'ma head out, Ms. Dorothea, but I promise to come back and see you again soon." I was already tossing my purse onto my shoulder as I stood.

"I know you're not tryna leave 'cause he came, when a second ago you was just cryin' about y'all relationship!" She frowned, giving me a look like she dared me to lie. My cheeks immediately heated after she put me on blast, and my eyes shot to him, hoping he had missed it, even though I knew it was stupid. He was watching me also, but with a blank expression, like Ms. Dorothea's confession didn't move him one way or another.

"Stop bein' messy and eat yo' food before it get cold, Dorothea," he ordered, taking a seat in the other chair.

"If it do, I'm gone send yo' ass to warm it back up! And tellin' the truth ain't bein' messy! It's obvious y'all need to talk, so stop avoiding each other and do that!" The whole time she spoke, she was digging into her bag and pulling out a small soup cup and spoon.

"Uhh—"

"She made her choice, ain't nothin' to talk about," he cut me off, and I could feel him staring a hole in the side of my head while I kept my eyes on Ms. Dorothea. "Ain't that right, Cam?" His tone had me pissed off and I chuckled bitterly, turning to see if he was serious, and he was.

"Yeah, I did, but I wasn't the only one makin' choices either, so stop actin' like you ain't done anything wrong because we both know that's a lie!" I fumed, wanting to jump across the bed and slap the stupid look off his face. I'd been in there trying not to throw him under the bus even though I had every right, and his ass wanted to make it all about me. Ms. Dorothea was eating the drama up right along with her soup as he stood towering over me and her.

"Don't be in here lyin' on me in front of my granny! I ain't did shit to yo' crazy ass! You decided to leave and I let you! That's it, that's all!"

"Yeah, and you know why I did, but I sure as fuck didn't know you been taking yo' lil' crackhead ex out on dates!" I barked back, enjoying the look of dread that crossed his face, and it made me laugh bitterly. "How long that shit been goin' on, hmm? You're a big ass hypocrite, and to think, I was bouta call you and try to work shit out, only to hear y'all giggling over an expensive meal!"

He opened and closed his mouth, knowing damn well he didn't have an argument, and that only had me more pissed off. "Well, you gone explain yo' self or what? We ain't got all day!" Ms. Dorothea interjected, looking upside his head like she was just as mad as me.

"It ain't shit to explain! Ain't shit sexual about what I got goin' on with Tania and you know that! Stop tryna make it seem like it's something it ain't! Don't nobody want that girl. Shit, I wanted yo' ass, but you ran as soon as some shit went down, just like she did!" he hissed with his chest heaving, and I slapped his pointed finger out of my face.

"Don't be comparing me to that bitch! She ran, I just wanted some time to get my mind right and I immediately regretted it, but you had already shut down on me and I wasn't bouta beg you to talk to me!" I choked on my words as Ms. Dorothea opened up her sandwich, and a wave of nausea hit me so hard that my stomach lurched. Before I had us all covered in vomit, I slapped a hand over my mouth and ran into the en-suite bathroom, barely making it over the toilet in time. For the next few minutes I threw up everything in my stomach until there was nothing left and I sat dry heaving. When I finally stopped, I leaned back against the wall trying to regroup and catch my breath, when Dinero came in.

"You ayite?" he questioned, handing me one of the white towels from the rack. Snatching it, I helped myself off the floor and swayed dizzily. "Woah, woah, woah. Sit down before you bust yo' damn head." Rushing to my side, he held me up while he dropped the lid on the toilet and flushed it before helping me to sit.

"I'm fine, clearly I just need to go home, 'cause being around yo' lyin' ass is making me sick." I didn't need to be so mean, but at this point I couldn't help it. Instead of backing off, though, he wet another one of the towels in cold water and folded it across the back of my neck. Despite my attitude, I couldn't deny that it felt amazing.

"Chill out, man," he said, eying me like he was trying to figure out what was wrong just from looking, before filling one of the disposable cups with water and handing it to me. "You need to be tryna find out if yo' ass got food poisoning or some shit instead of tryna argue with me."

"That girl ain't got no damn food poisoning, Dinero! She pregnant!" Ms. Dorothea hollered from the other room with a chuckle, and my heart immediately dropped. I thought back to the last time we'd had sex the night they left, panicking at the possibility before shaking my head in denial. We'd had slip-ups before and my period still came on like clockwork, yet I'd never gotten sick. Suddenly, another wave of nausea hit me and I hurriedly jumped up and dry heaved into the toilet again while Dinero stood by grumbling. When I finally got control and sat back against the wall, he leaned down to eye level with a serious look on his face. "Clean up, we need to go get a test."

CHAPTER ELEVEN

DINERO

The last thing I was expecting when I dropped by the hospital was for Ca'Mahri's ass to be there, but it was like Dorothea had special powers or some shit. She always knew everything about everything, and it seemed like the shit was more potent in her old age. I had no doubt that she had a hand in us running into each other up there and couldn't nobody tell me different. She was way too happy to get us arguing and then drop the pregnancy bomb on my ass. While Ca'Mahri was trying to think of reasons why she wasn't pregnant, I knew better than to try and question her. If she said we were about to have a baby, then we were about to have a baby, it was as simple as that. She was still in denial even as we rode to the nearest Walgreen's for a test. I wasn't going to try and convince her, though, I'd let a positive test do that for me.

"You don't need to come in, I can handle picking one out." She was already taking off her seatbelt. Instead of arguing with her ass, though, I took mine off and took the key out so she knew I was coming too. That instantly had her sucking her teeth in irritation as she climbed out, and I caught up with her

at the front of the car, unfazed. It was crazy how I'd just been
dead set against even seeing her, but now since I was in her
presence I couldn't leave her confused ass alone. I trailed
behind her, unable to keep my eyes off her juicy ass bouncing
in the bright yellow sundress she wore. I was sure she hadn't
even put much effort into her look, but the average person
wouldn't be able to tell. She was looking so good I had to mean
mug a few of the male employees and customers that were
eyeing her lustfully.

Coming to a stop, she browsed the section where the tests
were housed, reading the front of different boxes like they
didn't all say the same shit, and I ran a hand down my waves
with a sigh. I didn't know shit about which ones were better or
more accurate, but I figured the most expensive one should do
the trick. She was still looking when I snatched three of the
ones with the highest price tags and gripped her hand up in
mine.

"These the ones, let's go."

"How do you know I want those ones?" she huffed sassily
as I pulled her toward the checkout lines. "Stop! I said I don't
want those ones!" Stopping abruptly, I spun around and
looked down at her with narrowed eyes.

"Chill the fuck out, bro, you're actin' like a lil' ass kid! This
shit is really just a formality, because we both already know
but you obviously need to see it with yo' own two eyes! Stallin'
ain't gone make this any less real!"

"Fine!" she pouted childishly, avoiding my eyes, and I just
shook my head before continuing to the register with her
lagging behind me. I was already going through my own shit
about having another baby and didn't have time to deal with
her tantrums. It was fucking with me not knowing how she
was going to react once the truth was staring her in the face. As
bad as I wanted to just wash my hands of it so I wouldn't have

to deal with being crushed for the second time in my life, I couldn't just walk away.

After paying, I tried to hand her crybaby ass the bag but she refused to take it and instead stomped off toward the car. I shook off my irritation and decided to let her make it as I climbed behind the wheel and tossed the bag into her lap anyway. I'd barely gotten out of the parking lot when my phone started going off, and the screen showed it was Tania calling. Ca'Mahri instantly folded her arms and leaned back against the door, burning a hole in the side of my head. Smoothly, I sent that shit to voicemail, ignoring her sucking her teeth beside me.

"You ain't have to send yo' lil' girlfriend to voicemail for me, or did you not want her to know you was in the car with yo' possible baby mama?"

"I know a muhfucka who broke up with me ain't questioning me about another bitch. You better be careful, a nigga might think you actually give a fuck," I teased, taking my eyes off the road long enough to catch her rolling her eyes and waving me off.

"Tuh, you wish I gave a fu—wait, where you goin'? My house is the other way." Her brows dipped.

"Camille's house is the other way." I shrugged, unbothered by her obvious displeasure. She immediately began talking shit, which didn't faze me in the least. I was taking her ass home to do the test and since she'd rode with me, there wasn't much she could do about it.

When I pulled up in front of the house, I wasted no time getting out and going around to get her door, but she remained seated with her arms folded. I hadn't ever experienced her being so damn difficult and I hoped it wasn't a symptom of pregnancy, because if she chose to keep the baby I wasn't trying to deal with that shit for nine months.

"Man, get yo' ass out and come on before I help you out," I scoffed, quickly growing tired of her antics.

"I wish the fuck you would touch me!" Sighing, I reached in and unsnapped her seatbelt, lifting the bag, then tucking my arms behind her back and underneath her legs simultaneously. I lifted her with ease despite her pushing against my chest and wiggling her legs.

"You gone be feeling shitty if you fall tryna act up!" I warned as I walked up onto the porch. Being stubborn, she continued to fight and somehow I managed to get us inside, dropping her as soon as I kicked the door shut behind me.

"Asshole!" Grumbling, she pulled at her dress, straightening it out, then snatched the bag out of my outstretched hand.

"Gon' get to it, you know where the bathroom at." I was already heading toward the living room but stopped when I realized she still hadn't moved from the foyer. "You need some help or somethin'?"

"Ughhh!" she huffed, storming off. I noted with a smirk that she decided to ascend the stairs instead of using the half bath that was just down the hall. Clearly, she still considered this her home to an extent and after her confession at the hospital, that shit had me feeling good as I got comfortable in the living room and cut on the TV. It was rare for me to have some downtime to just chill at the crib. I was always in a rush to run here or there for one reason or another. Then again, I may have been avoiding my house because Ca'Mahri hadn't been there. I'd gotten used to coming home to her and sleeping with her plump ass pressed up against me. Sitting there, I couldn't help but acknowledge how good it felt to have her back, even if it was for a little while. The shit had me considering what Cash had suggested and I had to laugh at myself, just as my phone went off again. My smile instantly fell at the sight of Tania's name on my screen. As uncomfortable as I was having this conversation with her, I knew I couldn't continue to put it off.

"What's up, T?" I answered, watching to make sure Ca'Mahri wasn't on her way back into the room.

"Dinero?" Her voice came through mousy like she was surprised.

"Yeah, it's me. I'm kinda in the middle of something tho', so..." I hunched my shoulders like she could see me, ready to just get this shit over with.

I could almost feel her disappointment through the phone before she spoke. "Oh, well I was just calling to apologize about what happened. I was reading your signals all wrong and I don't want it to affect our friendship because I really appreciate you being there for me."

"It's cool T, I ain't trippin' 'bout that lil' shit. You always gone be my homie."

"You sure? 'Cause you've been avoiding all my calls and you haven't been back to take me to lunch either. I was hoping Ca'Mahri wasn't upset and maybe keeping you away." It was obvious she was trying to fish for information. She wasn't privy to what had happened between us, but I was sure she'd gathered that there was something going on when she'd ask about Ca'Mahri and I'd shut the conversation down. I didn't want to think she was being messy, but it seemed like it.

"Nah, we've just been busy out here workin' and shit. Sometimes it just takes more of my time than others," I lied easily.

"Well—"

"I'ma have to get up with you later, ayite." The sound of Ca'Mahri's sandals clicking down the marble stairs had me rushing to hang up before she could even speak. Dropping my phone in my lap, I tried to look casual like I hadn't just been on some sneaky shit, just as she came around the corner. It may have just been my paranoia, but it felt like she was burning a hole in the side of my head.

"Were you just on the phone?" she questioned, inching into the room and sitting on the very farthest end of the couch.

"Yeah, just some business shit." I didn't try to hide my amusement at her trying to sit so far away.

"Mmhmm....well the tests said to wait three minutes so we got about two more to go." We sat in an uncomfortable silence with just the sports channel playing in the background. I tried not to get my hopes up but the closer my watch got to the time, I couldn't stop my mind from wondering. Exactly two minutes later her phone went off and we both stood at the same time. It felt like my heart was pounding out of my chest as I walked behind her to our bedroom. She had all six tests laid out on the sink in the bathroom, and she immediately reached for the one closest to her before moving down the line. Her reaction had me picking one up even though I already knew what it said. With a sigh, I stood propped up against the wall waiting for her to speak.

"So?" I asked, watching as she leaned over the sink with her chin touching her chest, before she turned to me with watery eyes.

"I guess we're bouta have a baby."

CHAPTER TWELVE
CAMILLE

S o much had happened in such a short amount of time that I almost missed my doctor's appointment. My growing stomach had me anxious because it was beginning to look like it might've been twins in there stretching me out. Cash would've just loved sitting my ass down with twins and Kash, but that was far from what I was looking forward to. It was already hard getting used to the idea of just one baby and if I found out there were two, I'd probably fall into a deep depression.

"You almost ready?" I must have spoken him up because he ducked into my bedroom and his eyes lit up with lust, taking in my body in the short jumper I was wearing.

"Nope, don't even try it. We don't have enough time for that." I locked eyes with him in the mirror of my dresser, already shaking my head.

"Try what?" His brows dipped as he came closer, pressing up against my butt. I could already feel his hard dick poking me and I knew I was about to lose the battle.

"Caaash!" I whined, barely putting up a fight as his hands roamed my body.

"What, I'm just makin' sure you ready." He sucked my earlobe into his mouth and simultaneously eased his hand in the waist of my panties. My body jerked roughly as he spread my lower lips and pinched my sensitive nub. Any chance I had of leaving the house without having to change immediately went out the window the second his finger dipped between my silky folds. "See how wet you is? These definitely need to come off." With ease, he ripped my lace cheekys from my body and continued to push his fingers in and out of me.

"Baby, hurry up!" I moaned, hearing him unbuckle his pants over the sound of his digits playing in my wetness. I was on the verge of exploding when he snatched his hand back. With his head down, he licked them clean before running them between my ass cheeks. I'd already began leaning over my dresser, but he pressed down on my back, creating a deeper arch.

"Ssss, fuck!" he hissed, sliding into me slowly. I could feel him all the way in my stomach, but that didn't stop me from grinding against him since he had yet to move. "Damn girl, slow yo' ass down. This shit too wet."

"I know you ain't start somethin' you can't finish?" I teased, smirking at how weak my pussy always had him. Pregnancy had me wetter than the ocean and always ready to fuck. My sex drive had definitely surpassed his, but he was always willing to oblige me.

"Oh, you tryna talk shit?" His face hardened with determination, and he gripped my hips as he pulled out and slammed back inside me. There wasn't shit I could hold onto to steady myself with the way he had me positioned, so I crossed my arms on top of the dresser and rested my head against them.

"Mmm baby, you so fuckin' deeeeeep!" I whimpered, trying not to reach back to make him ease up.

"Good! You was talkin' all that shit like you ain't know what this dick could do! Don't complain now!" He smacked my ass, leaving a stinging sensation that hurt so good I shuddered.

"Shit, right there! Right there!" He'd bent his knees so he could go deeper, and the constant tapping of my G-spot had me convulsing as I came. My nut didn't slow him down at all; instead, he massaged my asshole with his thumb, knowing how much I liked that. I was so wet that I could feel it dripping down my legs. The only sounds that could be heard were of him slipping through my wetness, my moans, and an occasional grunt from him. My eyes rolled into the back of my head as an orgasm tightened my stomach and my knees almost buckled.

"Shit, I'm bouta nut all in this good ass pussy!" The words were barely out of his mouth when he squeezed my waist tightly and thrust into me one last time. I could feel his dick still throbbing as he shot his seeds inside me, and I clenched my muscles making sure to milk him. "I'm gone have to keep yo' ass pregnant! God damn!"

An hour later, after we'd both showered and changed, we pulled up to the doctor's office grinning like fools. I didn't know if it was good dick he'd just delivered or how fine he looked in his joggers and wife beater, but I was feeling super in love. It was no doubt that my baby daddy had my mind gone, and I realized that I'd easily slide a bitch over him, which was crazy because I *never* considered fighting over a nigga. For Cash Banks, though, I was willing to beat a bitch silly. The thought had me giggling as he held the door open for me to step inside the ice-cold building.

"Fuck yo' ass giggling about?" He grinned cockily, falling into step beside me and catching my hand.

"Nothin', just thinkin' 'bout how dizzy I am over yo' black ass." Just saying it out loud had me chuckling and shaking my head.

"Aww, I love yo' apple head ass too, baby," he confessed, giving me a quick kiss. My heart fluttered in my chest and I felt myself blushing. As we approached the receptionist desk, the lady behind the counter looked up at us smiling widely.

"Oh my! Well, aren't you all just the cutest!" she gushed, only making my cheeks heat more. This wasn't the first time we'd gotten complimented while we were out together and it never got old.

"Thank you." I couldn't help beaming. "I have an appointment with Dr. Bennett at 1:30."

She continued to shower us with compliments as she asked for my date of birth and other information to sign me in. Once she finished we found a couple of empty seats in the waiting room. It wasn't that packed, which I was happy about, but the few women who were in there were having a hard time keeping their eyes to themselves. Thankfully, they called us back right away before I messed around and cursed one of them out.

After the initial check of my height, weight, and blood pressure, we were left alone to wait for Dr. Bennett. Cash didn't waste any time being nosy and looking through the cabinets and drawers. "I swear, I can't take yo' ass nowhere! Sit down, boy!" I tried to sound serious, even as I laughed at his crazy ass. Before whatever smart shit he wanted to say could come out, there was a knock at the door and Dr. Bennett peeked her head in.

"Good afternoon! I take it you're Dad?" she questioned Cash, who kneed the drawer closed that he was looking into, and I was instantly embarrassed by his nonchalance. There wasn't any type of urgency about the action either as he came over to shake her hand.

"Yeah, Cash."

"Well, it's nice to meet you Cash." I breathed a sigh of relief since she hadn't said anything to his ignorant ass about snooping and smiled as she greeted me. "It looks like you've grown a lot since the last time I saw you! You sure you're not having twins?" The question had my smile falling instantly, while Cash laughed like the shit was funny.

"Nah uh, Doc, don't even play like that."

"Okay, okay, well you are in your second trimester so it's not unusual for you to be showing like this. Let's check on baby and see." After she listened to the heartbeat and talked to me for a little bit, she sent us down to get an ultrasound and I was more than excited because if the baby behaved we'd be able to find out what we were having.

"You ready for this?" Cash asked, sitting next to me as I laid back on the exam table waiting for the ultrasound tech. He was unusually calm, cool, and collected, and I attributed that to him having done this before. It was easy to feed off of his energy, though, which put me at ease because I couldn't help being a little nervous. There was no telling what we would see, and I just prayed that our baby was healthy.

"Hi Mom, hi Dad! I'm Janet, and I'll be taking your photos today!" The ultrasound tech fluttered into the room cheerfully. "I see we're going to be finding out what baby is today!"

"Hey, hopefully they act right," I said, looking at Cash who just shrugged. I really hadn't thought about what I'd be having, but since we were so close to finding out I was suddenly thinking of buying girl things.

"Well, even if baby decides to give us a hard time, I do have a few tricks." She winked, pressing buttons on the machine.

"What type of tricks? Don't hurt my baby tryna get a

picture of their genitals and shit." Cash mugged her and surprisingly, she chuckled.

"Cash!"

"Oh, it's okay honey, I've dealt with a worried father or two," she let me know before turning to him. "I promise nothing I do here today will hurt the baby. Sometimes they're a bit stubborn so to get them to move around we can try something sweet, juice, even rubbing the belly to promote movement."

"Oh okay, I can fuck with that." His ignorant ass nodded and kissed my hand like he wasn't doing the most. I gave him the evil eye while Janet tucked paper towels into the top of my pants and squirted a bunch of warm gel on my belly.

"Okaaaay, I'm going to check some measurements and then we'll have a photoshoot!"

Even though I couldn't see anything from where I sat, I still craned my neck to try and look at the screen. I was extremely thankful when she finally turned the monitor toward us and began pointing out different body parts and labeling them with the keyboard. Seeing my baby's little body had my eyes stinging with tears. I don't think I'd ever felt my heart so full as when I was able to lay eyes on the life growing inside of me. Cash looked just as emotional, and we simultaneously squeezed each other's hands.

"Welp, it looks like there won't be a need for any tricks today. Are you guys ready to find out what you're having?"

"Yes!"

"Hell yeah!" me and Cash answered at the same time, making her smile widen.

"Congratulations, it's a girl!" Since we really hadn't talked about what either of us wanted, I just assumed that he'd want another boy like most men, but the way Cash jumped up flashing all thirty-two of his teeth before kissing me let me know how excited he was.

A half hour later he was still cheesing from ear to ear as we drove back home. He'd even put one of the ultrasound pictures on his dashboard like a true proud father, and I couldn't lie, his vibe was infectious. Even I was unable to stop looking at the pictures I held in my hands, noting every small detail, and I made a mental note to buy a baby book so I could have somewhere to keep all my memories.

"You know I love yo' fine ass, right?" he blurted as we stopped at a red light, and I squirmed in my seat, both horny and blushing from his sudden affection.

"Awww, I love you too, bae," I said, adjusting my seatbelt so I could lean over and give him a kiss that quickly turned from a quick peck to him devouring my lips, until horns started blaring.

"Aye, shut yo' bitch ass up, I'm tryna love on my baby mama!" his crazy ass shouted out the window, and I couldn't do shit but shake my head. No matter how sweet he could be, he would still turn up on anybody. "What?" he quizzed when he realized I was laughing.

"Nothin', crazy ass boy." Unfazed, he placed another kiss on my lips before finally pulling off just before the light turned yellow.

CHAPTER THIRTEEN
CASH

S hit had been going so well that I'd put all the negative shit on the back burner even though I knew that wasn't the move in our line of work. After finding out about having a little princess, though, I couldn't bring myself to tell Camille that her pops was a pill popper. She was still riding the wave of being a girl mom and the last thing I wanted to do was bring her down. She loved her daddy and would no doubt be devastated to know he was abusing drugs. For now, the easiest thing to do was not mention it, but sooner or later I'd need to come clean.

It had been almost a month since her doctor's appointment and I'd been planning some special shit for her. I even got our families involved, I just needed to get her suspicious ass to go with the flow. I made sure I chose a day when she'd be off so I knew she was home just stuffing her face and watching TV. That was exactly what she'd been doing when I'd left earlier that day. I told her I was going to be working at the funeral home, but really I was with our families getting shit set up for her. As soon as I stepped in the house I could hear her yelling at the TV, and I laughed to myself.

"That nigga did it, even I can tell!" she hollered, and I knew her ass was in the room watching some crime show, probably *Snapped* since that was her favorite. Wanting to scare her, I crept up the hall to her cracked door silently. I paused just outside the door and listened before busting it open. Shorty jumped so hard I thought she'd hit the ceiling, and I instantly fell out laughing.

"Ahhh! God dammit, Cash! Why would you do that!"

"My bad, bae, but yo' ass wouldn't be so scared if you wasn't always watching this shit! My baby bet not come out tryna kill niggas for their life insurance 'cause of yo' ass!" I joked, but I was dead serious. It wasn't a whole lot I knew about babies, but I knew at some point they'd be able to hear and I ain't want her hearing no psycho shit.

"You worried 'bout the wrong one comin' in here like that, asshole!"

"Awww, my baby mad, I'm sorry." I came around and crouched down, trying to kiss her as she pouted and avoided my eyes. Glancing at the candy wrappers scattered near her, I raised my eyebrows. "What it's gone take for you to not be mad? You want some food? I'll get whatever you want."

That was all it took to have her face brightening, and she quickly swung her legs around to the floor. "Okay, and I want extra everything too!" Seeing how fast she got up for some food had me shaking my head, but I was gonna let her make it since my baby was partially to blame. I took in what she was wearing and as usual, she looked good in a nude, two-piece lounge set that hung off her shoulder, putting her luscious skin on display and showing off her round belly. Even her hair was done in a high curly ponytail with bangs hanging on each side.

I stood back watching as she slipped her feet into some furry slides and tried to resist the urge to get a quickie in.

"Aht, aht, put yo' tongue back in yo' mouth, you ain't gettin' none!" she teased, sticking her tongue out at me childishly.

"Damn, I can't just admire yo' sexy ass?"

"Nope!" I just chuckled as she grabbed her little bag and started toward the door with me right behind her. The way her ass was filling out her pants, I couldn't stop myself from copping a couple of feels on the way out the door, but she slapped my hands away every time. She definitely had an attitude, but I knew by the time we made it to our destination that shit would be gone.

Helping her into my truck, I went around and got behind the wheel, driving out toward our estate while she busied herself on her phone trying to avoid talking to me. Normally, I would've been fucking with her, but I wanted her attention off of our destination because as soon as she saw where we were headed she was going to know something was up.

"Okay, I wanna go to Sugar Factory," she suddenly announced, barely looking up as I agreed and passed every exit that would've taken us there. I guess she realized we'd been driving straight for a while and finally looked out the window. "Where we goin'? I'm hungry, Cash."

I bit back a smile at her whining and sighed like I was irritated. "My pops texted me to come see this crib he tryna flip. You know this his first one so his old ass need advice." It was hard as fuck not to give shit away when I saw the saddened look on her face. I knew her greedy ass wanted to protest, but she settled to show her unhappiness with a grunt, folding her arms under her breasts.

We were pulling up a short time later and her eyes narrowed as we passed our estate. "Yo' daddy bought a house right across the street?" She frowned, looking past me to our property before settling back in her seat with a shake of her head. "This some rich people shit for real. I guess you get to pick yo' neighbors at least."

"Yo' ass rich too, but handpicking the people who live near you is definitely a flex," I agreed, making my way up the long driveway. The way the house was set up you couldn't see it until right before you hit the end of the drive, and the look on her face was priceless. While her jaw was dropped in awe, I grinned proudly, knowing that she'd be even more amazed once she saw everything else.

"Damn! Is he sure he don't wanna keep this one for hisself?" I'd barely stopped the truck and she was already climbing out so her nosy ass could go inside, making shit easier than I thought.

"Slow up, man, how you gone leave me?" I teased, catching up to her and grabbing her hand up in mine. When we got to the door, I encouraged her to go ahead and open it. As soon as she crossed the threshold, she stopped. Both of our families were standing there in a sea of red rose petals that stretched from the foyer and down the hallway. We even had white glass candles placed in different corners of the room in sets of three. Hundreds of red balloons with matching ribbons draped over their heads from the ceiling, and the contrast against the white that covered every other inch of the space gave it the perfect romantic vibe.

Camille's hands flew to her mouth as she looked back and forth between us before I nudged her further inside. "Welcome home, baby," I said lowly, removing her hands and wiping away the tears that were streaming down her cheeks. Her eyes bucked and she looked around again in disbelief before turning back to me. "You don't wanna step foot in that house again, cool. This is a fresh start for us, somewhere you don't have to relive nothin' fucked up, or sleep on yo' wack ass mattress. Just say the word and it's yours."

"Hell yeah!" she shouted, making our family laugh as she jumped into my arms. Laughing from the way she was hanging on my neck like a chain, I carried her across the floor.

"Marry us, Amille!" Kash shouted, and his little voice echoed around the empty mansion. Her head shot up immediately, almost busting my nose as I sent a hard stare my son's way.

"Nigga, you too early!"

"And nigga, you too late! Hurry yo' ass up and get to it before you burn this damn house down with all this flammable shit!" my pops snapped, looking around uncomfortably.

"These muhfuckas," I grumbled, shaking my head at my family's antics as I pulled the velvet ring box from my pocket. Setting Camille's feet on the floor, I dropped to one knee as she trembled, already nodding her head. "I guess this whole shit outta order since you already sayin' yes before I even ask."

"Stop talkin' shit boy, damn!" my mama was next, cutting in while Dinero chuckled.

"Kendrick, bro, get yo' wife man!"

"I got mine, you need to get yours, hell! Long as you takin' she gone fuck around and change her mind!" This shit had turned into a whole session of us talking mess to each other and I wanted to kick myself for hiring a nigga to tape it when it was going to be full of bloopers and shit.

"It's okay, baby, go ahead," Camille voiced, drawing my focus back to her with a stroke to my cheek. It was like I could see her body buzzing in anticipation.

"I can't even lie, you're the best thing that ever happened to a nigga. You match my crazy, you love on my son like he's yours, you check my ass when I'm outta pocket, and don't nobody regulate shit like you," I said, making us both laugh.

"That's right, baby!" her mama shouted.

"Now you givin' me a baby girl too. I couldn't imagine my world without you in it and I damn sure don't want to. Say you in this shit with me forever." I was finally able to finish my speech with no more interruptions and cracked open the ring box to show her the ten-carat, heart-shaped diamond engagement ring I'd splurged on.

"Of course, I will!" Her hands shook as I slipped it on her finger, being careful not to drop that expensive muthafucka. After giving me a hug and kiss, she was pulled away by her girls. I couldn't help but grin as my pops, Dinero, and their father came over patting me on the back. I was out here making big moves, shit I wouldn't have even been thinking about a year before, but now that I had, there wasn't any turning back.

CHAPTER FOURTEEN
DINERO

It was crazy watching my little brother man up right before my eyes. Considering he was the main one that wasn't trying to settle down and only wanted to run through hoes, I had to admit I was proud of him. He had me ready to go look at some rings to see if I could wring Ca'Mahri's tough ass back in. Since finding out she was pregnant, she hadn't been giving me too much of a hard time but she wasn't trying to move her ass back home either. It was getting to the point where I was beginning to consider locking her ass up like Cash had suggested since obviously the shit worked for him and Camille's crazy ass.

I was a different type of nigga, though, and not nearly as toxic as my brother was so that shit didn't really work for me. I sat in our rental office going over numbers and contemplating whether or not I should call her and see if she wanted to have lunch. Knowing her, she'd have some smart shit to say about me and Tania but after thinking about it, I went ahead and dialed her number.

Hey, Dinero," she answered breathlessly like she'd just ran

a marathon. My forehead immediately creased wanting to get in her business, but to keep the conversation from going left I didn't.

"What's up, how you feelin' today? You good?" From what I knew she hadn't really gotten a lot of morning sickness since that first time, but I still wanted to make sure since we didn't talk as often as we should've.

"I'm okay, I guess." Her words came out slow like she was trying to figure some shit out.

"Good, good. I just wanted to check on you and my baby and make sure you're good while I got some down time... You uh, you hungry? We can go grab a bite, my treat," I offered.

"I, umm, actually have my first appointment today so I was going to skip lunch and—"

"Why I ain't know you had an appointment, the fuck!" All that keeping the peace shit went out the window immediately. I could somewhat understand her reservations about getting too close to me, but keeping me out of the loop when it came to our baby was some shit I wasn't going to be having. The awkward silence on the other end had me even more pissed off as I snatched up my keys and stood.

"They told me it wasn't really an important one. Just confirming the pregnancy and checking my cervix, Dinero. I didn't think it was going to be a big deal," she said stupidly, and I wished I could reach through the phone and choke her ass Homer Simpson style.

"I don't care if they only want yo' ass to come piss in a cup! If it got somethin' to do with my baby, I wanna be involved!"

"You're right. I guess I just assumed you wouldn't want to come, and I shouldn't do that. If you're not busy now, I'll send you the address so you can meet me up there." Even though I caught her in time, I was stilled pissed and her apology only irritated me more.

"Gon' do that. I'm headed out the door now." I hung up before she could respond and stopped to tell the secretary that I'd be out for the rest of the day. From the look on her face I could tell she'd heard a little of my conversation, well, at least the part where I was yelling and cursing, and she was clearly uncomfortable. She nodded quickly and ducked her head back into whatever she was working on. If I wasn't so focused on getting to Ca'Mahri's appointment then I probably would've tried to reassure her that I wasn't crazy, but I really didn't have time for that.

I was climbing behind the wheel of my Camaro when the text finally came through with the address and directions for once I got to the building. Typing it into my GPS, I pulled off breaking all types of traffic laws. I cut a forty-five-minute trip in half and whipped into the parking lot and parked in the first spot I saw, which happened to be a few feet from the door.

Checking the time, I saw that I had a little less than ten minutes before her appointment and I slowed down a bit. After locking up my car, I shoved my phone and keys into my pockets then started to cross the lot, passing a couple of pregnant women on the way.

"Goood damn! If I wasn't pregnant I'd sholl be tryna get at his fine ass!"

"Shiiit, it's stepdaddy season so a lil' belly don't matter!"

I shook my head but kept walking, until I was face to face with Ca'Mahri, who was waiting for me at the door. Just from the way her mouth was twisted up, as she looked past me to where the women had gone, I knew she'd heard them talking.

"What them wobbling ass bitches say?" she questioned as soon as I was close enough.

"Man come on, you got like five minutes to get yo' ass in here and you worried about some random pregnant muhfuckas when you the only pregnant muhfucka I'm tryna get up in." I ushered her ass back into the building and to the elevator, finding it hard not to laugh at her fake jealousy since I was supposed to still be mad.

Once we stopped on the third floor, I held the doors so she could step out first and then followed her to the desk. While she checked in, I looked around appreciating how clean and nicely decorated it was. There were posters of the body during different stages of pregnancy and other informational things hanging on the walls. The waiting area was full with only a few chairs available to sit, and I hoped that meant the doctors were good there because I wouldn't hesitate to find a new one for her.

The check in went fast and after she filled out a little sheet we found a couple seats along the back wall. While we waited I checked a few emails and handled some other business stuff on my phone, avoiding the eyes of all the women that were staring like they weren't either there with somebody or pregnant by somebody. By the time a nurse came out calling her to the back, half of the waiting room was empty. I realized that a lot of them were waiting on labs and had already seen the doctor, so we didn't have to wait long.

In the back they checked her weight and height, then sent us into a small room where the exam table was. I listened intently to the conversation so I was aware of anything that may have been wrong or if I should have been paying attention to anything specific when it came to her. Other than her blood pressure being a little high according to the nurse, everything else seemed to be on track. She asked a few more questions then told Ca'Mahri to remove her bottoms and get on the table before breezing out of the room.

"Aht, don't look." Ca'Mahri had begun to pull her leggings down when she realized I was watching and stopped abruptly.

Leaning back in my chair, I folded my arms behind my head and smirked.

"I done seen everything you got, Cam, and you pregnant so ain't no need to hide now."

She folded her arms and raised a brow at me. "Nigga, you act like I won't get you put out of here. You wanna be involved, fine, but you don't gotta be in the exam room to be involved," she sassed.

"Yeah ayite, make me cut up and show you me and Cash share the same blood." I wasn't playing either. She hadn't really seen me do too much, but if she tried to get me put out the room I was going to tear some shit up. We had a stare down for a few seconds before she finally sucked her teeth and took off her leggings and panties swiftly, like that was going to stop my view. "See, that wasn't so hard," I teased as she climbed onto the table, careful to not let me see too much before unfolding the cloth in her lap.

She looked around the room awkwardly trying to avoid my eyes, but that didn't stop me from ogling her. I'd heard that pregnancy enhanced a woman's beauty and it had no doubt been benefitting her. Unable to take the silence any longer, I stood, crossing the small space so that I was standing in front of her.

"What are you—" she blurted, tensing up.

"I thought I heard you call me over here," I lied, finding the wrinkle in her nose sexy. I may have just been horny as hell since I hadn't seen any pussy since she gave me some at the penthouse. Either way, just being that close to her damn near naked had my dick pressing against my jeans.

"Now you know damn well—"

"You don't want me over here, Ca'Mahri? Tell the truth, I know yo' ornery ass miss me." My hand was already underneath the paper and sliding between her smooth thighs. "Open up." There wasn't any room to object my demand and her legs slowly inched apart, giving me full access to her hairless pussy.

"Dineroooo," she moaned, and I grinned proudly. She was definitely just as backed up as I was because I'd barely touched her clit and she was already dripping on the paper underneath her.

"Can I taste it?" I asked, licking my lips in anticipation as I swiped my fingers between her lips.

"Please." *God damn!* That was enough to make me do some shit I hadn't done since I was a little nigga, and that was bust with no penetration. Pulling over the doctor's stool, I sat down and lifted the paper like I was opening up a fucking present on Christmas, coming face to face with her slick center. I immediately dove in, latching on to her clit and alternating between sucking and flickering my tongue.

"Ohhh my god, baby, fuck!" she squealed, looking down at me with her face twisted in pleasure. She fell back and I lifted her legs so that her feet were planted on the table, giving me more access. I tongue kissed her pussy before probing her hole with my tongue as she screeched and tried to pull away.

"Nuh unh, you been keepin' this good ass pussy from me for too long. Keep still so I can catch every drop," I ordered, pulling her closer to the edge so her ass was hanging off. The way I had her ass in my hands devouring her juices reminded me of eating a watermelon, and she was just as messy.

"Dinero, I'm bouta nut! Oh my god! Oh my—" Rubbing my head, she grinded against my face faster and faster until she released a loud ass noise as her body jerked, soaking my beard with her wetness. She twitched as I continued lapping up every bit that I could until she was clean. With a grunt I adjusted my dick and stood, swiping my face before reaching down to help her back into a sitting position. She was still whimpering as I dropped a wet kiss on her lips. We were so deep into it that I was ready to fuck her right there, when a knock at the door had her jumping and almost taking my damn tongue with her as she snatched away.

The nurse ducked her head inside, eyes darting between the two of us suspiciously before she finally spoke. "Sorry about the wait folks, the doctor had a patient go into labor so she had to rush to the hospital, but we do have Dr. Reese that can finish your exam unless you want to reschedule with Dr. D."

"We can wait," we both answered at the same time, already preparing to finish what we'd started as soon as she left the room.

CHAPTER FIFTEEN
CA'MAHRI

After we'd cleaned up with some of my Honey Pot wipes, I finished my exam and was able to get an ultrasound. Our baby looked like a little bean with arms and even though I'd been on the fence at first, seeing it had put everything in perspective for me. Or it could've been the amazing work Dinero had done with his tongue. I shuddered just thinking about it as I shoveled a forkful of chicken alfredo into my mouth.

"I know that shit ain't that damn good." He eyed me quizzically from across the table. Since I was starving after my appointment, I decided to take him up on his offer for lunch. I immediately chose Olive Garden because I'd been craving the creamy cheese noodles for a couple of days and it definitely hadn't disappointed.

Chewing, I rolled my eyes and prepared another forkful. "Actually, it is. Beanie baby likes it." I shrugged, causing his face to scrunch up.

"Who the fuck is Beanie baby, yo' imaginary friend? 'Cause I know you don't think you callin' my son that shit!"

"I meeeeeaaan, it fits. And you don't even know what we're havin' yet so the nickname don't matter," I reasoned, not wanting to argue, but I would if he was going to spend months trying to automatically assign me a son. I'd be happy either way, but I didn't want his ass swaying the odds by speaking a boy into the universe.

"Yeah ayite."

Waving his ass off, I continued eating before pointing to the empty spot in front of him. "You sure you don't wanna get somethin'?" I asked like I was the one paying. Sitting back, he smirked devilishly and rubbed his belly.

"Oh, I'm full still." He licked his lips and my clit thumped imagining them wrapped around it. I was sure that he was fully aware of what he was doing, and even as I rolled my eyes I found it hard to hide the grin on my face. I couldn't believe that we'd just been at each other's throats and now we were sharing a meal...well, I was eating while he watched.

"You're so nasty." Shaking my head, I looked down at my half-finished plate.

"I meeeeaan, you fed me so you nasty too," he teased, using my words against me with a shrug. Before I could reply his phone rang, and I instantly rolled my eyes when he sent it straight to voicemail. "Don't trip, that was just some work shit." He must have noticed my mood shift and tried to explain, but it was too late. Regardless of what he'd told me about him and Tania, having heard them flirting that day on the phone had me on the defense.

"You could've answered it. You don't gotta ignore work because of me." I shrugged, trying to hide my attitude. Him suddenly being sneaky with his work calls when I was around was new to me, and even though I figured it was due to our recent breakup it still bothered me.

"Nah, they're straight. Besides, I'm not answering *for* you," he clarified, and my nose scrunched, not liking the sound of that, but he quickly held up his hands. "I mean I'm tryna spend time with you right now, them muhfuckas can handle whatever's goin' on. That's what they're gettin' paid for anyway." I relaxed a bit but didn't speak, opting to just nod as I continued eating.

"You want anything else?" he finally asked, breaking the silence that fell on the table. Eating my last bite, I shoved my empty plate away and shook my head. I was stuffed, honestly, and I couldn't even make room for dessert.

"Hell no, that pasta has me too full. Now I just need a nap." I'd left school then went straight to my appointment and the activity of the morning was beginning to take its toll. A yawn slipped out further proving my statement, and Dinero chuckled.

"Ayite. You wanna take some dessert home?" I hadn't been thinking about it but as soon as he said something cheesecake came to mind.

"Ummm, I could handle some cheesecake," I said, and we both laughed before he waved our waitress over and ordered my cheesecake to go.

Fifteen minutes later we were walking to our cars and as soon as I went to open the door to mine, he pushed it back closed and pressed up against me, planting his arms on either side of my head. Like clockwork butterflies filled my stomach from his proximity. Shit, even my breathing was different. He lowered his head so that our lips were damn near touching too. "Let me come take a nap with you."

"You ain't slick, nigga. If you in the bed with me the last thing you're gonna be doin' is tryna sleep," I accused, and he grinned, letting me know my assumption was right.

"I can't make any promises, but I'll try to keep my hands to myself." My lips twisted in disbelief even though I already knew I was going to be staying with him.

"And yo' tongue?" I quirked a brow, and his grin widened.

"Yo' ass drive a hard bargain, but if it means I can get you home then I'll see what I can do."

"See! Nope!" I was already turning like I was about to leave, but he quickly stopped me.

"Ayite, ayite! I'ma be cool." I looked at him in mock skepticism and he laughed. "Come on man! Just meet me at home, ayite?" He gave me a soft kiss then opened the door so I could get inside and closed it back once I was behind the wheel. It was obvious he was talking about the home we'd shared so I headed toward the estate.

Dinero pulled up behind me and we both got out at the same time. He was already cheesing at the fact that I really came as we met up at the door and he let us in. "Let me get that." Taking my cheesecake out of my hands, he disappeared toward the kitchen and I made my way upstairs. I wasted no time going in the bathroom and stripping out of my clothes for a shower. The wipes were good but they were no match for soap and water. All of my things were still exactly how I'd left them and I couldn't stop myself from swooning as I lathered and washed a few times then rinsed off. Wrapping a huge black towel around myself, I entered the room and was surprised to find it still empty. That was better for me anyway, because I didn't want to further entice my baby daddy. After moisturizing I pulled on an oversized shirt and a comfortable pair of shorts.

The bed was made up with my pillows all over just like I always did it, and I tossed them off to make room before slipping under the plush comforter. I sunk into the soft mattress, already feeling so comfortable that I closed my eyes. It felt a whole lot better than anything at Camille's house and I had to admit, I missed sleeping there.

I was on the verge of unconsciousness when the bed dipped and Dinero's fresh scent filled my nose. I must've actually dozed off because he'd obviously taken a shower himself. As soon as he laid down and wrapped his arm around me, I instinctively snuggled even closer, making him groan.

"Keep playin', I'ma give you what you beggin' for, Ca'Mahri." The warning didn't do anything but make me settle deeper into his lap. I could already feel his dick beginning to grow as I grinded against him and he bit into my neck roughly.

"Mmmm," I moaned lowly, reaching back and caressing the back of his head as he attacked my neck. His hands were roaming all over my body and unable to take it anymore, I turned to face him, catching his lips with mine.

We'd quickly gone from preparing for a nap to fucking for hours and before I knew it, the sun had gone down. The way Dinero handled my body had me in post orgasmic bliss. I laid there watching him as he slept, and thinking of whether or not I was ready to come home, when my phone rang. Seeing my mama's name wasn't unusual, so I climbed out of bed to answer her.

"Hey Ma—"

"Ca'Mahri, you better come over here and get yo' daddy before I kill his ass!" she shouted, cutting me off, and I could hear him fussing in the background. I immediately perked up and started throwing on my clothes. It had been a long time since I'd witnessed my parents fighting, but even hearing it through the phone as a grownup, I was on high alert.

"What happened?" I wanted to know as I moved around the room grabbing my purse and keys. That had Dinero's light sleeping ass up and watching me in confusion.

"Just come get him! *Now* Ca'Mahri!" She damn near busted

my eardrums before hanging up, and I blew out a frustrated breath. I for sure thought their toxic shit was behind them, but I guess it was always something.

"What's up? Where you goin'?"

"I need to get to my parents' house," I tried to say it calmly, but the truth was I was anything but calm. It had to be some serious shit to make my mama call and put me in their business, so I was thinking the worst. The worst being that their fighting had finally gotten physical.

"Ayite." Without any further questions he began to get dressed in some sweats and slides. I was nervous and it felt like my legs were noodles as we walked out to his car, and I was glad that he chose to drive because I didn't think I'd be able to.

He held my hand as we walked up to my parents' door, and I could already hear them yelling from outside. It sounded like my mama was standing right next to the door, and that was proven when she let us in after Dinero rang the bell.

"Good, y'all right on time!" She ushered us inside and pointed toward the living room. "His ass in there!"

"Ma, what's goin' on?" I quizzed, refusing to move until she told me something. With a huff, she stormed off to where my daddy was, forcing us to follow.

My daddy was in the living room on the couch surrounded by a lot of his belongings. He had his head in his hands, but as soon as he heard us coming he looked up with an expression I could only describe as embarrassment.

"Tell her! Tell yo' daughter what you been out here doin'!"

"Come on, Allani! You really puttin' them in our business? This ain't got shit to do with the kids!"

"Like hell it don't! You think you being a crackhead don't affect them? Huh? You're they're daddy and yo' ass on drugs! They need to know before you start stealin' shit for yo' next high!" My head had been ping ponging between the two but when she said that, I looked at my daddy with wide eyes.

"Is that true Daddy?"

His eyes bounced around the room and landed on Dinero, who'd been quietly observing everything, and I knew she was telling the truth. Instantly, my heart dropped into my stomach. That was the last thing I expected to be going on when I came over, but it definitely explained why my mama was so mad.

"Cam, I know it seems bad, but it's really not that big of a deal. It's just oxys and I really only take it when I'm havin' problems with my back—"

"Oh, it's a big damn deal! Is that where you got that black eye from not too long ago, talkin' 'bout a nigga tried to rob you? I should've known that was some bullshit! Niggas in Chicago ain't robbin' nobody with they damn fists!" My mama shook her head at the realization, while I was still reeling about the fact that he was popping pills.

"Shut the fuck up, Allani, damn!"

"You shut the fuck up and get this shit out my house before I burn it, hype!" His eyes damn near popped out of his head at the insult, and they began to bicker back and forth before Dinero finally got involved. I was going to have to start calling him the crackhead whisperer, because he convinced my dad to leave out with him while I talked to my mom. When he was finally out of the house, she broke down in tears and I had to try and comfort her while also trying to figure out how to help my daddy.

CHAPTER SIXTEEN
CAMILLE

"I just can't believe my dad on drugs." I sighed, shaking my head. Although my mama hadn't called me over there like she'd done Ca'Mahri, I'd still found out about the latest drama with our parents. I was still trying to figure out if there'd been any signs that I could think of and came up short every time.

"I mean, it's not hard to get addicted to pain pills though, bae, give the man a break." I was immediately skeptical about the way Cash was defending my daddy's bullshit, but figured it was a man thing or at the very least, he was doing it because of our close ties.

"I'ma give him a break alright, straight up to the rehab," I scoffed irritably. Dinero had put my dad up in a hotel for a couple of nights, but I would've preferred he took him to a damn facility instead. We were on our way to have some type of weak ass intervention, and I really didn't know if I'd be able to handle it. Throughout our lives our parents hadn't been perfect, but I'd always felt a strong connection with my daddy. Being the most like him out of us two made me his roady, and I relished our relationship. So, to find out he had something like this going on had me both pissed and hurt. When had this started? Why did he feel like things were so bad that he had to turn to drugs? Could I have helped? A lot of different questions were running through my mind and I couldn't stop my leg from bouncing in the passenger seat.

Sensing my anxiety, Cash put his hand on my thigh and gave it a light squeeze. "It's gone be okay, bae. It's early enough that he can get some help," he assured me, and I prayed that he was right.

We pulled up to the Hilton that my daddy was staying in and parked not too far from Dinero's bright ass car. When they spotted us, they got out and met us on the sidewalk with my mama walking reluctantly behind them. She looked like she'd been crying, but the look on her face was stoic as I walked over and hugged her.

"You okay Mommy?"

"Don't make me start crying again, Camille," she said stiffly and gave me a light pat on the back as she let me go. My emotional ass was already on the verge of tears just imagining how she felt in all this. "Let's just get on in here and get this shit over with." Straightening her spine, she walked into the hotel and Ca'Mahri and I shared a look before following with the guys behind us.

From the elevator, Dinero directed us to his room and we huddled at the door as my mama knocked. When he still hadn't answered after a few seconds, she knocked louder, only to get the same results, before Dinero stepped up.

"Hold up, I got the other key." He pulled it out and opened the door for us. My mama was the first one in the room and she immediately smacked her lips.

"This muhfucka ain't even sleep here!" She was already shaking her head as she headed back toward the door. "I'm sorry, I ain't bouta play these crackhead games with Darnell! If his ass wanna stay on that shit, he can, and I'll be filing for divorce!" She stormed out with Ca'Mahri right on her heels. Just like she said, the room was completely clean and it was obvious no one had been in there. Seeing that had me releasing the tears I'd been fighting to keep at bay.

"Fuck, don't cry, shorty. I don't want my princess stressed out, ayite. I'm gone find yo' pops ayite, don't worry," Cash promised, and without a doubt, I believed him.

He dropped me off at my parents' house where my mama and Ca'Mahri were while he went with Dinero to find my daddy. By the time I got there my mama already had a glass of some dark liquor in her hand.

What the fuck! I mouthed to my sister, who was sitting on the couch, and she just shrugged her shoulders. It was obvious my mama was going through it to be drinking so early in the damn morning.

"Come on in here and help me find a divorce lawyer since yo' sister don't want to." She waved me over once she saw me enter the room. The drink clearly had affected her thinking, and I rolled my eyes, taking a seat next to Ca'Mahri on the couch. "If you not gone help you could at least have a drink with me, Cam!"

"Ma, it's too early for all that," she said with her nose turned up, and my mama smacked her lips dismissively.

"Ma, why don't you come sit down so we can figure this out?"

"Ain't shit to figure out besides what lawyer I wanna go with! Ain't you supposed to be on Google or Safari or whateverthefuck looking for me?"

"Girl, I ain't bouta help you leave my daddy over one mistake! At least give him a chance to make it right!" I argued, not liking how quickly she was giving up on him. No matter

IN THUG LOVE WITH A CHI-TOWN MILLIONAIR... 105

how shocking it was to find out, I was sure there were worse things my daddy could've done to warrant a divorce.

"Actually, I gave his ass a chance this morning and just like a crackhead, he chose drugs over his family!" She narrowed her eyes at me and I looked to Ca'Mahri to help, but her ass was looking sick to her stomach.

"Okay, but—"

"No buts, Camille! You only just got engaged, girl, so you all freshly in love, but there are some things that are unforgivable and jeopardizing our family is one of those!" She paused long enough to finish off the corner of liquor in her glass and walked over to their mini bar grumbling. I had to admit, I was slightly offended by her mentioning me and Cash. Our relationship wasn't the issue, but I knew that if anything like this was to happen to us, I'd be willing to help him and not immediately throw him aside. Frustrated, I turned to Ca'Mahri's quiet ass for some help, only for her to slap her hand over her mouth and run out of the room. We could hear her in the bathroom down the hall sounding like she was dying, and my mama looked at me with her forehead scrunched.

"What the fuck?"

"Don't look at me." I shrugged. Instead of going to question her like I wanted to, I stayed on the couch so I wouldn't fuck around and get sick myself. Cash's little rude ass daughter had only just recently stopped giving me crippling morning sickness and I wasn't trying to rock the boat. I had questions, though, and if we needed to, we'd be taking a trip to the pharmacy.

A few minutes later Ca'Mahri came shuffling back into the living room looking tired and avoiding our eyes, before taking her seat next to me. "Uh, do we need to go get a test, 'cause what the fuck was that?"

"Uh, yo' mouth, girl!" my mama chastised, snapping her

fingers at me, and I resisted the urge to laugh, choosing instead to apologize before putting my attention back on Cam. "Well?"

Sighing, she looked at us uncomfortably, then reached into her crossbody and came out with a piece of paper. "Surprise! I'm pregnant!" she said, flipping the paper to reveal an ultrasound.

"Awwww! Congratulations!" I cooed, pulling her into a hug.

"Oh, my goodness! When did you find out? Why didn't you say nothin'?" My mama rushed over, seemingly sobered up.

"It's only been a couple of weeks, but I wasn't trying to take Camille's shine. I was gonna tell y'all, but it seems like stuff keeps gettin' in the way. I guess this baby said it's time to spill the tea."

"Aww, you could've told me. I'm happy to be sharing the spotlight with you! Now our babies can grow up together!" I hugged her again, unable to contain my excitement. Finding out my sister and me would be experiencing motherhood together had me geeked. I could already imagine us shopping together and our daughters dressing alike on holidays. The news immediately lifted the mood and changed the topic of conversation, which was great because anything was better than talking about our mama divorcing our daddy.

Hours had passed and it'd turned into a regular visit minus my daddy being in the wind, but I was just happy my mama wasn't drinking and grieving anymore. After finding out about Ca'Mahri being pregnant, she insisted on feeding both her grandbabies and proceeded to start cooking. Even though I knew her behavior was all over the place, I let her make it, partly because I was hungry but mostly because she needed something to keep her mind off her problems. While she cooked us up some fried chicken, dirty rice, and broccoli, Ms. Keisha showed up as even more emotional support. They'd gotten reacquainted and had been in communication with each other ever since the barbeque.

She was just as surprised as we were about Ca'Mahri's pregnancy and even though they hadn't been seeing eye to eye after the breakup, she was extremely receptive. The day had been steered in a totally different direction from where it started, until a call from Cash interrupted me stuffing my face. I was still chewing when I rushed to answer, hoping he had found my dad.

"Hey, did y'all have any luck?" I questioned immediately, and my heart dropped hearing him sigh.

"Yeah, I'ma send you the address," he told me. Just from the sound of his voice, though, I knew it wasn't all good news. I just hoped it wasn't anything that could further destroy our family.

CHAPTER SEVENTEEN
CASH

It was becoming difficult for me to focus on finding Lox because shit just kept popping up. Shit with Camille's pops was just another issue I felt the need to take care of along with Dinero, since my baby mama's happiness took precedence over everything including revenge. It was far from over, though, and I'd be making sure to put a bullet in his head.

It wasn't very many places for us to look for Darnell, but we knew more than likely he was somewhere drugged out. I wanted to kick his ass for the confusion he'd caused that day, but that would only upset Camille even more. There was already the issue of Dinero and me knowing about the shit and not saying anything. He'd told us about getting addicted to pills after a back injury but he swore to get help. Being who I was, I should've never believed the word of an addict, but that shit hits different when it's close to home.

"Gone in there and get yo' father-in-law," Dinero said, smirking once we pulled up outside of the bar that Mason had tracked Darnell to.

"Jealous ass nigga."

His goofy ass laughed, unfazed, as we climbed out. "I ain't gotta be jealous of shit. As you can see, me and Cam good again, plus she bouta have my baby, so I'm in there nigga!"

"Whaaat? Let me find out you got on some Cash shit and trapped her ass with a baby!" Now it was my turn to crack up. "I knew you had it in you!"

"Man, fuck you, ayite. Unlike yo' ass, I ain't gotta do all that crazy nigga shit!" He dismissed me as we stopped at the bar's door so a couple people could leave.

"I mean, whatever helps you sleep at night, muhfucka!" He could pretend if he wanted too but my methods worked. As soon as we walked inside, Darnell was one of the first people we saw sitting at the bar. The empty shot glasses lined up in front of him let me know he was probably barely holding himself up on the stool. He looked around like he sensed us or some shit. The second his bloodshot eyes landed on us, he rolled them and waved over the bartender, pissing me off.

"Aye, can't you see his ass don't need no more? The fuck kinda bar is this, ain't yo' ass supposed to refuse people that's obviously fucked up?" I sneered, rushing up to stop the blonde bartender from filling another glass for him. She looked like she was ready to say something and I dared her to with my eyes, prompting her to suck her teeth and walk off.

"Gon' now, Cash, my night been bad enough." Darnell swayed, keeping his eyes on the wood of the bar like he was trying to study that shit.

"You think it's bad, nigga, yo' wife bouta divorce yo' ass! You need to clean yourself the fuck up and come with us to get some help before you lose yo' wife, yo' kids, and yo' future grandkids, 'cause I damn sure ain't lettin' my shorty around yo' pill poppin' ass!" Dinero shot a look my way and I did the same. I didn't know what he expected, but I wasn't about to coddle his ass.

"Look Darnell, what my brother tryna say is that your family needs you, and sittin' here at this bar ain't gone do shit but push you farther away from them. I mean, damn, you told us you were going to be gettin' off that shit."

"I don't gotta answer to y'all lil' niggas! Y'all part of the problem but wanna come in here harassing me! Shit, I probably done bought something off one of y'all—hey!"

I was tired of going back and forth with his ass and quickly snatched him up by the shirt. It was nothing to lift him off the stool, and Dinero immediately looked at me ready to discourage me from dragging his ass out. Ignoring him, I pulled that nigga out the door while he hollered and talked shit.

"Aye, chill before you have these muhfuckas tryna call the police and shit," I said, shaking him a little as we walked to the car.

"Let me go! I'm not ready to leave yet!" I could see I was going to have to beat their daddy's ass out there, which I was trying to avoid, but I didn't have the patience for this shit. Frustrated, I tossed his big ass in the backseat and slammed the door closed while my brother stood off to the side shaking his head.

"You know he just gone try to get out on the other—"

"Help me! This nigga crazy!" Darnell slurred, trying to climb out the other door.

"Fuck! Man, get in the back with his ass while I drive," I told Dinero after I'd gotten him back in the car. His ass was standing around silently judging my methods instead of helping, but he reluctantly did what I'd said.

The whole time I drove he was yanking on the door handle and yelling for us to let him go. He finally passed out slumped up against Dinero, and I resisted the urge to call to let Camille know we had him. I knew she was gonna be sick if he took his ass in there acting like that. My baby was already fucked up over his drug use, so to find out that he'd run off to get high and drunk instead of waiting on his family was a blow I didn't want her to take.

Instead of taking his ass home I took him to the crib Dinero and I used to count money. I pulled into the garage so none of the neighbors would see us carting his big ass inside and cut the engine. This time Dinero helped me carry him in and straight to the shower stall. We cut the cold water on hoping to wake his ass up, and then I went and started a pot of coffee.

It took a good couple of hours for him to seem somewhat sober, but along with that came a bunch of emotions that I wasn't trying to deal with. He was crying nonstop long after we'd gotten him out the shower and changed into some old sweats we found.

Shaking my head, I blew out a frustrated breath as I watched his ass cry over his cup of coffee. He was clearly just going to spiral and needed a professional, because I wasn't prepared for that shit. I called Camille and told her we had him then text her the address. The way her mama was talking earlier that day I didn't think she'd come, but when they pulled up she was right there along with my mama.

"Get yo' ass up, Darnell!" she ordered as soon as she laid eyes on him. I guess he hadn't heard them come in, but the second he heard her voice he jumped up and wrapped himself around her body.

"I'm sorry, baby! I'll do whatever you want me to, just don't leave me!" He had already started crying again, and she pet his shoulder trying to comfort him.

"You need to go get help and then we can talk about us being together," she said matter of factly, and he quickly nodded to agree.

"Okay, okay! I'll do whatever you want!"

"Well, let's go right now then," she wasted no time saying, and we all watched to see what his response would be. Of course, he agreed, and she wasn't playing either. She immediately told the girls to say their goodbyes to him because she was about to drive his ass right then.

I kept a close eye on Camille to make sure she was good but besides a few tears, she handled herself well. Their mama refused to let them tag along to go drop him off because she didn't think it would be good for them considering that they were pregnant, and I agreed. We all watched them get into her car to leave and I just hoped that nigga didn't disappoint them.

A week later it was time for my granny to be discharged and we all piled into her room while she fussed about us making it a big deal. It was good to see her old ass back to her usual funny self, but we were all still worried. Seeing her laid up in a hospital bed was hard on us and regardless of her saying she was alright, it had me on edge.

"Boy, get back and give me fifty feet! I don't need all this fuss!" she hollered, swatting at me as I tried to adjust her feet onto the footrest.

"Dorothea, bro, don't be hittin' on me. I'm just tryna help."

"Go help yo' fiancée out that cake and leave me the hell alone!" All eyes landed on Camille, who had been in the corner picking off of the cake we'd brought to celebrate, and we all laughed at the startled look on her face.

"What? Y'all wasn't gonna finish it," she pointed out, frowning, and I just shook my head at her greedy ass. My baby had her eating more and more and it seemed like every time I looked up, she was shoving something in her mouth.

"Man, get yo' ass from over there feeding my baby all that sugar! I don't wanna hear you whining later on when she tryna kick her way outta there either!" I grumbled, watching as she shrugged and waved me off.

"I'm bouta carry this stuff downstairs then I'll come back to wheel you down, Mama," my pops said, trying to juggle some of the many flowers we'd been bringing her, but she instantly shook her head.

"Hell naw! Leave all them flowers and shit here for the next patient. I don't want all them things taking up space in my room!"

"Ayite, I don't wanna hear you complaining about leaving all these pretty flowers behind." He set them down and went to get behind her chair, only for her to stop him.

"Okay, well maybe we can take the roses at least," she quickly backtracked, making him chuckle as he directed me and my brother to start gathering her stuff, flowers included. My mama stood by holding Kash in her arms like he was a damn baby, before following my pops and granny out of the room.

"Oh, I can carry that." Camille jumped up when I came over to grab the cake, and I couldn't help but laugh.

"Fuck it, come on." She lifted the pan from the table it sat on and carried it out with me right on her heels. Instead of laying it across the backseat, she held it in her lap as we drove back to my parents' house. Since Granny was returning, we had a special dinner planned and my pops had called in a chef that cooked meals catering to people with specific diet needs. According to him, the man was a beast in the kitchen, and you couldn't even tell his food was missing any of the things we loved that weren't good for us. I just wanted to see what Dorothea's reaction would be if that food was anything other than delicious. After being in the hospital for so long eating their nasty food, she'd probably pull out a belt out and beat my pops's ass if he paid a chef for a nasty ass dinner.

I pulled up right after my brother and went around to open the door for Camille. Like the true food feign she'd become, she struggled to climb out and hold onto the cake at the same time. "Leave that shit in here girl, they got dessert inside." Pulling her in the house, we were immediately met with the smell of something good cooking and were directed to the dining room where everybody was beginning to sit.

They were already bringing in the food and I watched my granny scrutinize each dish with a hard stare. I couldn't lie, it didn't look any different than the usual food we ate, so I didn't know why she was looking all crazy and shit, but it was funny as hell to see.

"Here Ma, try some of these potatoes." My mama was shoveling different things on her plate while she looked on with her nose turned up.

"What kinda potatoes is this? All this shit smell funny," she tried to whisper, but I was sure everybody at the table heard her loud and clear. A sharp look from my mama stopped my laughter immediately, before she put her attention back on my granny.

"It's nothin' wrong with this food, Ma. Kendrick, tell yo' mama the food is good."

I missed whatever my pops said because my phone had stolen my attention. I'd been waiting on a word from Mason and I'd finally got it. That nigga had found Lox.

CHAPTER EIGHTEEN
CA'MAHRI

W hen I made it to the house after my classes, the last thing I wanted to do was have a get together, but I sucked it up for Ms. Dorothea. It was good to see her out of the hospital and back in her element, checking everybody left and right.

"Hey y'all!" I greeted everybody when I entered the dining room, not seeing Dinero, Cash, or Kendrick in sight. I came around and gave Ms. Dorothea a kiss on the cheek and took a seat on the other side of her.

"Hey baby! They tricked you into comin' to eat this mess too, huh?"

"I wish you'd stop sayin' that. Ca'Mahri, I've tasted everything on this table and it's good," Ms. Keisha said, looking around Ms. Dorothea so she could give me a pointed look. I really didn't know who to believe, but judging from how nobody else at the table was touching there's, I was more inclined to side with Ms. Dorothea. Even little Kash was picking around his plate instead of eating like normal.

"She lyin', Cam," Ms. Dorothea warned, eyeing me as I

rubbed on some hand sanitizer and put a little of everything on my plate, not trying to be rude despite me believing everything Ms. Dorothea was saying.

"I'm not bouta argue with you, old lady." Ms. Keisha waved her off and went back to eating her own food.

"'Cause it ain't no argument. You're the only one eatin' and yo' own sons and husband done left the table so they wouldn't have to eat it."

"You know that's not why they left, Ma."

They continued arguing while I pushed food around my plate so that it looked like I'd been eating. I'd already made up in my mind that we were going to order something once we left. Thankfully, the heavy breakfast I'd had was holding me over, because there was no way I was going to attempt the food on the table.

The fuss that Ms. Dorothea was making over the food had Ms. Keisha having a salad brought out to her. That seemed to somewhat satisfy her since she was already aware of her dietary limits, but I still had to stop her from shaking a bunch of salt over the lettuce. We were damn near done by the time the guys reentered the room with unreadable expressions.

"How y'all feel about a weekend trip?" Cash finally broke the silence with a grin. My eyes immediately found Dinero's and he just shrugged. Something about a random trip out of town had me on edge, and it was probably because the last time I'd let him take me out of town things went left.

"Don't trip, we got some business out in Vegas so we figured we might as well take y'all too and turn it into a vacation," he said, sensing my unease. I hadn't ever been to Las Vegas, but it was one of the places I'd always wanted to visit. Being pregnant would make it a little less fun since we couldn't drink, but I figured we could still do some gambling.

"When we leavin'?" Everybody was talking excitedly as the

guys filled us in on the plans, and I relaxed a little knowing that we would all be going.

"Early tomorrow since y'all off for the weekend. So, after we eat we need to go start packing," he explained. Since the day of my appointment, I'd basically moved back in with Dinero. Besides the fact that I'd missed him, he'd been a big comfort after finding out about my dad.

"Oh, I'm done!" Camille and I said at the same time, making Ms. Dorothea crack up laughing at how fast it had come out. The whole time my sister had been picking at her food just like me, which was saying something because she was greedy as hell usually, but I'd only seen her take a bite, if that.

"You know what, get y'all asses out my house! I tried to get a healthy meal prepared for y'all and y'all being rude!" Ms. Keisha snapped, folding her arms over her chest.

"Baby, I love you, but we might've fucked up with this one." Mr. Kendrick was trying hard to keep a straight face as he reached for her hand, instantly making her snatch away.

"Get off me!" she grumbled, getting up from the table and leaving with him following behind her trying to plead his case.

Once the maids came to clear the table and take Ms. Dorothea away, we got up to head home. I was already planning what I'd wear while we were gone, but that quickly turned from four outfits to eight, just in case I changed my mind. Unlike me, Dinero didn't have any trouble coming up with a few things to wear that would work for any occasion, and he was finished within an hour of us starting.

"Why you tryna take so much? It ain't like yo' ass can do shit but eat and maybe play some slots." He chuckled, looking from me to my full suitcase, and I raised my middle finger at him.

"It's plenty of other shit I can do. I can go swimming or to the mall, see some shows—"

"Maybe get married?" Frozen, I looked over at him trying to see if he was serious, and his thoughtful expression quickly spread into a grin. "I'm just fuckin' with you, I wouldn't do you like that, bae."

"I'm glad you know 'cause I'm not settling for anything less than the works when it comes to my wedding day, and a nigga dressed up like Elvis ain't gone cut it." We'd already had this conversation and I'd hate to have to go upside his head for trying me, pregnant and all.

"I mean, they do got other impersonators out ther—"

"Dinero, stop playin'!" I whined, stomping my foot irritably.

"Ayite, ayite." He was still laughing like I was a joke, when his phone rang. Right away the smile disappeared from his face and a look of confusion replaced it. Sitting up, he slid the bar across the screen to answer, and I could tell he was receiving some bad news. "Ayite, I'm on my way." He was up and moving around the room, gathering his stuff to leave, only informing me that he'd be back.

"Uh, who was that? What's wrong?" I'd stopped packing and was now following him out of room and to the door. It was obvious he was going to try and leave without telling me shit, and I wasn't going for that. I pressed myself between him and the door, stopping him from going out of it. "You can't just leave like this without tellin' me where you're going, Dinero!"

"I'm goin' to the hospital. The rehab said that Tania tried to fuckin' kill herself." I was more than shocked at that piece of news, and my mouth opened and closed a couple times trying to think of what to say.

"Wha—how? Why would she do that?" I fumbled over each question, trying to wrap my mind around what he'd told me. Even though I hadn't been in contact with him regarding her I didn't think that she was doing so bad she'd want to die, and I instantly felt bad.

"I don't know, but I'm bouta go find out."

"I'm comin' too then."

"Nah, stay here, you still need to finish packing. I can handle this," he refused, trying to not let the hurt in his voice be heard, but I was already shaking my head no. As many times as he'd been there for me, I wanted to return the favor.

"No, I'm not gonna let you go by yourself. I can finish packing later." I didn't even wait for him to agree or not, I just slipped on my shoes and pulled the door open. "You comin'?"

It didn't take us long to get to the hospital where she'd been taken, and as soon as we walked in a lady noticed him and immediately reached in for a hug. "Dinero, I'm so glad you made it. They're working on her right now." She looked at me for a minute before returning her attention to him.

"What happened, how was she able to harm herself when y'all were supposed to be watching her?" He didn't even attempt to hide his displeasure, and the woman's eyes bucked at the hostility there.

"Well, we have hourly rounds where we do a head count and all of them accounted for her until the last one. The security found her in the tub with her wrists cut." Gasping, I squeezed Dinero's hand as his shoulders drooped. I'd never known anybody who had tried to take their own life and despite how much I didn't fuck with the girl, my heart went out to her. She went on to tell him that they'd immediately went to revive her and brought her to the hospital. After they'd reviewed her phone, it showed multiple calls to Dinero, and they figured she'd done it because he hadn't answered for her. I didn't know how to feel about that because technically, he hadn't done anything wrong, but did that mean it was his fault? He instantly spazzed on her, though, and she backed away fearfully. The remainder of the time that we stayed there she stayed on the other side of the waiting room and I felt like that was in her best interest, because there was no way I'd be able to stop him from tearing shit up. He spent the next hour with his head down until the doctor emerged and called for the family. Since we were the only ones there other than the woman from the rehab, we all huddled around and awaited the news, but before he could even speak his face gave it away.

"I'm sorry, but there was nothing we could do." My eyes immediately shot to Dinero and I couldn't read his expression. It was a cross between rage and despair, and I couldn't help being worried that he'd do something crazy. I was surprised, though, when he calmly spoke with them about getting in contact with him for burial plans, before guiding me back to the car. The ride home was a silent one. I didn't know what to say and at that point I didn't know if there was anything I could say, so I just held his hand. No doubt guilt was probably eating him alive, especially after finding out she'd done it after trying to call him.

His demeanor was scarily calm, as we made it home and he disappeared into his office while I went to unpack my suitcase. A deep sadness had come over me and it had nothing to do with our trip seemingly being canceled. I just felt bad for both Tania and Dinero, and my previous issues seemed so trivial at the moment.

"What you doin'?" Dinero's voice sounded behind me as I made a trip to the closet to return some clothes, and my forehead bunched. He hadn't necessarily told me that the trip was canceled, but it was assumed following such a terrible event.

"I, uh, I thought we weren't going anymore," I mumbled, and he shook his head stoically.

"Nah, we already had these plans. I can handle the shit

with Tania when we get back. Finish packing, I got some calls to make," he said, leaving me stunned into silence. I really didn't know what to make of the way he was acting, but if continuing on like things were okay helped for now, I'd play along. I just hoped he wasn't having some type of psychotic break or some shit.

CHAPTER NINETEEN
DINERO

Finding out about Tania had me fucked up and I didn't know how to take it. Unfortunately, my feelings had to go on the back burner because we had a location on Lox and it was time to put his ass down. I guess my lack of emotions was making Ca'Mahri walk on eggshells around me, even though I kept trying to tell her I was okay. She still watched me like she was just waiting on me to do some crazy shit, but that wasn't going to happen. My number being the one that Tania tried to call before she killed herself did make me feel guilty, but it wasn't like there was shit I could do. She wanted something from me I wasn't willing to give and so I had to create some distance. Her actions only further proved that I'd been right to do so.

"Ahhhhh, biiiiiitches!" Noelle made her presence known before we even saw her loud ass and immediately, Ca'Mahri and Camille ran over to her. Knowing that the business we were going to handle would leave them on their own most of the time, I'd invited her to keep them company. I just hoped her crazy ass didn't have them too turned up.

It was still early as hell when we landed so after we got checked in at the hotel, the girls went to see the strip with a couple of guards they didn't know were with them. It probably seemed crazy, but being in a different state and with them being pregnant, I'd rather be safe than sorry. As soon as they were gone, though, we began tracking Lox. We were too smart to do anything in broad daylight, but we still needed to find the best time to actually snatch his ass up.

Mason ended up finding him because the goofy nigga applied for a new phone out in Vegas. He figured he was safe since his name hadn't come up in any news back in Chicago, and that was a big mistake. It wasn't shit for Mason to hit his ass with a virus that gave us access to his direct location. We pulled up to a dingy hotel far away from the strip, that was seedy as fuck. It was obvious only sex workers and drug addicts frequented that spot, and I was sure he was only there trying to save money.

It took about an hour before he emerged from his room and walked down to a beat-up ass Mustang. He had to have not been worried about us at all because he didn't even check his surroundings before getting in and pulling off with us right behind him. We followed him to an apartment complex where a half-naked woman came to the door and pulled him inside. I had to admit, I was surprised that he'd found some pussy that soon, but he was a fuck nigga, so pussy was always on his mind.

"Let's go grab something to eat right quick, that nigga obviously gone be a while," I suggested, and Cash quickly agreed, probably only because we wouldn't lose track of him. We drove up the street to a family diner and sat down in one of the back booths. Almost immediately, a waitress came over with menus and poured us some water.

"They called about Tania yet?" he cleared his throat and

asked while we browsed the menu. Considering that it was only the next morning, I wasn't expecting them to, but I still shook my head.

"Nah." I left it at that and set my menu down, folding my hands on top of it. I wasn't ready to talk about Tania or anything involving her at the moment. Mostly because my focus was on Lox, but even after we took care of him, I probably still wouldn't be ready. Sensing that I wasn't trying to have that conversation right then, he dropped it and checked his phone as the waitress approached.

She took our order, smiling extra hard before switching away. Cash followed the movement with a frown, and I knew it was killing his ass not to say anything. "Flat booty ass bitch. If she come back over here rattling them bones again, I'ma treat her goofy ass!"

He wasn't lying. The blonde-haired waitress was a straight up bag of bones and looked like her clothes were going to fall right off her. His facial expression had me cracking up despite my mood.

"Man, leave that damn girl alone!"

"She needs to leave us alone before I do her ass like ole girl on *Scary Movie 2*!" he grumbled, taking a sip of his water, and I damn near choked on my spit. "I don't even know how her lil' ass gone carry our damn food out, fuck around and throw her balance off." That nigga talked shit all the way up until she brought our food out and just like he said, she was wobbling the whole way to our table. She barely made it, but the way Cash narrowed his eyes at her had her walking straighter. I was surprised by how good my food looked and couldn't wait to taste it.

"Oh, shit! That nigga leavin'!" Cash was already moving to get out of the booth while I continued trying to shovel eggs in my mouth.

"He ain't goin' nowhere we don't know about, bruh. Sit yo' ass back down so we can eat first, nigga, I'm starvin'," I said irritably. I was cool getting a read on that nigga before we murked his ass, but I was going to eat first.

"Nigga, fuck that bland ass food! Let's go!" He tossed a couple bills on the table and walked off. Knowing he'd leave me if I didn't get my ass up, I cursed and climbed out of the booth, still eating from my plate. "Not you stealin' them people's plate." He shook his head and pulled off.

"I told you I was hungry, muhfucka."

I ignored the look he gave me and emptied the plate before setting it on the backseat. It didn't take long before we were parking at a liquor store where we caught Lox walking back out to his car with a couple of bags. Halfway into following him, I realized that nigga was heading right back to the bitch's house he'd left, and I mugged Cash's stupid ass. I knew there was something up with him leaving old girl's house so soon, and if I had left my food I would've beat his ass. Now I was ready to just bust in there and kill both of them, fuck it being daylight.

"Shit, my bad." He shrugged, smirking, and I waved his goofy ass off as I sent a text to Ca'Mahri. I needed a distraction and I wanted to know if she was having fun since I was busy. My phone immediately lit up with a FaceTime call, and I straightened in my seat before answering.

"What's up, shorty?" It was hard to resist smiling just seeing the excitement on her face.

"Hey bae," she gushed, and I could hear her loud ass sister and Noelle in the background. "We just left the wax museum and I got so many pictures! I wish you would've come too. You know they got yo' girl Beyoncé in there." She giggled and I immediately cut my eyes at Cash, who was looking right back at me. I'd fucked around and told her I fuck with some of the woman's music and she wouldn't let me live it down.

"Beyoncé, nigga?" he cracked, looking at me sideways.

"Shut yo' ass up!"

"I'm sayin', that *Lemonade* shit slap, huh?" His jokes had Ca'Mahri and the other girls giggling like fools.

"Man, I'm bouta hang up on yo' ass!"

"Okay, okay!" She laughed, changing the subject. We talked for a little bit longer and I was glad that she didn't ask me how I was doing. So far everybody had left the topic alone, but Ca'Mahri always felt the need to try and check in with me emotionally, which I loved most of the time but at the moment, it wasn't what I wanted. After talking to her I hit up their security to make sure they were doing what they were supposed to and keeping a close eye on them.

"If this nigga don't bring his ass on, I'ma just say fuck it and kill both them muhfuckas," Cash grumbled after we'd been sitting out there for a couple hours, and I raised a brow. I'd been clocked that there weren't any cameras outside shorty's crib. There was still a chance that the car we were in could be identified by a neighbor or some shit.

"I mean, we can catch him at the motel. You know ain't no cameras around that shit and ain't nobody over there gone talk." I could tell he really didn't want to let that nigga out of his sight, but following him around all day wasn't going to do shit.

"Bet." He nodded and pulled off. We still had at least seven hours before the sun went down, and whether his ass was at the motel or shorty's spot, he was dying that night.

Eight hours later

We'd spent the last few hours with the girls, going shopping and then out to dinner before heading back out. Periodically we checked Lox's location to see if he'd had any movement and thankfully, he'd finally left old girl's apartment. Despite the shit I'd talked earlier I was glad he'd moved around because technically, she was innocent regardless of the company she kept.

"Don't go in there doin' nothin' stupid, bro. Let's just get his ass out and take him out to the desert," I warned Cash, already knowing there was a chance he wasn't going to listen to shit I said. Being that close to the nigga that had stolen Kash was sure to make him fly off the handle, but I was hoping he'd try to have some self-control. "I—"

I was still trying to talk when he jumped his ass out of the car, and I cursed under my breath before slipping out after him. He was already at the door about to knock when I pushed him aside.

"You know he ain't gone answer the door for no nigga, and he definitely won't answer if he can't see!" I whispered, looking around and spotting one of the women working the area nearby. A low whistle had her switching our way, and I quickly flashed a hundred-dollar bill in her face. She plucked it out of my hand and knocked on the door lightly while me and Cash stood out of view.

"Aye, get yo' ass away from my door!"

"I'm just tryna see if you got any party favors, my regular guy is missing. Pleeease, I got money," she whined, and after a few seconds the locks clicked. Pushing her out of the way, our guns were right in his face.

"Oh fuck!"

"You got that right." Cash laughed and cracked his nose under the butt of his gun. "I been lookin' for you, muhfucka!" Tossing me the keys, he snatched Lox up by the neck and forced him to the car in only his boxers and a T-shirt. He rode the entire way in the backseat to a spot we'd scouted out in the desert where his body would never be found.

"Ayite man, look, I'm sorry! Shit just got outta hand but I ain't tryna die behind this!" he cried as Cash forced him to his knees.

"See, I was gonna make yo' bitch ass suffer, maybe cut off each one of yo' limbs. Unfortunately, I don't have time for that, and it really don't matter anyway 'cause as long as you're dead then I'll be able to sleep better every night. You should know, tho', that you don't deserve a peaceful death. Matter fact, fuck it." He emptied his clip in that nigga's head, splattering his brain across the cracked ground. "Come on bro, we still on vacation, right?"

CHAPTER TWENTY
CAMILLE

ONE YEAR LATER

I could feel myself getting misty eyed and I blinked rapidly to keep the tears at bay. "Aht, aht! Don't you fuck up this makeup, bitch!" Noelle stopped patting my face and narrowed her eyes at me.

"You're in a church, hoe, you can't be cursin' and shit!" I chastised. "Dang, now you got me cursin'! You gone mess around and make God curse my marriage before it even get started!"

"Girl, boom! God knows my heart, ayite, and if yo' marriage get cursed it's gone be because of Cash worrisome self! I bet he somewhere in here cursin' as we speak!" I rolled my eyes but couldn't stop the laughter from bubbling up in my throat. There was no doubt that Cash was somewhere around the church raising all types of hell.

"I know y'all heffas not in here talkin' 'bout my baby." Ms. Keisha came and stood next to us with our five-month-old daughter Karma on her hip. As soon as she saw me she started bucking to get out of her arms. When I didn't immedi-ately pick her up her baby babble turned into a holler that I was sure could be heard throughout the church. "Nope, get y'all's cryin' baby!" Ms. Keisha wasted no time handing her over and like the spoiled brat she was, she immediately stopped crying.

"Awww, she not a crybaby! Her just want her mama!" I cooed as I lightly rocked her. My baby was so pretty and chunky I could never get enough of her. Between me and Cash, I didn't know who was more obsessed with her, but he judging by the way she alternated her favorite, we were about tied.

"Girl, whatever helps you sleep at night." She sucked her teeth and walked out of the room, probably in search of Cash, no doubt.

"Look what you did, lil' fat girl. You hurt yo' granny feel-ings." I swear she rolled her eyes like she was unbothered and continued playing with the diamond necklace I wore.

"I swear she really be understanding yo' ass sometimes." Noelle chuckled, shaking her head. Honestly, I was sure she did too. Messing around with Ms. Dorothea had her acting like she'd been here before since she came home from the hospital. "Ok, all finished."

I sat up and closed my eyes while she misted setting spray on my face and began to fan until it was dry. "Finally!" It felt like I'd been sitting there for hours when really it'd only been one. My anxiety was high as fuck from all the people moving around and because it was my wedding day, so sitting still was a chore.

Since my hair and makeup were done I got up, propping Karma up on my waist since she'd slipped against my silk robe. It was still crazy that after the year we'd had we were getting married. Just thinking about it had me ready to cry again and I quickly fanned away the tears as Ca'Mahri came in holding her baby, DJ. He looked so cute in his little baby tux, and I hoped they made sure to take pictures of him.

"You look so pretty!" she squealed excitedly as her eyes grew watery.

"Thank you! So do you!"

"Thanks boo!" Noelle's crazy ass gushed at the same time as me, and I rolled my eyes, looking past my sister.

"Where's Kash?" I quizzed, wanting to see him in his little tux too. I already knew he looked so handsome that everybody in the church was probably trying to squeeze him.

"Dinero and them wouldn't let him leave with me, talkin' 'bout he had to stay with the men." She made her voice deep trying to mock them and sucked her teeth. The door didn't even close again before our parents were pushing it open. My dad looked better than he ever had and had been doing much better after finishing a sixth-month stay in rehab. Even though my mama had been insisting on a divorce, they'd started counseling after he completed treatment. From what I could see things were going well between them.

"Oh my goodness, you look beautiful!" My mama pulled me into a hug and immediately began sniffling. Even my daddy was ready to cry and I had to fight not to break down myself. It was going to be an emotional day and I needed to brace myself though.

"Don't make me cry y'all!"

"Okay, okay. You gon' back in there with the guys, Darnell, so we can help her get into her dress." She shooed my daddy away and dabbed at her face. Laughing, he gave me a light kiss on the cheek before doing the same to Ca'Mahri and then pecking my mama on the lips.

"Alright, I love y'all and I'll see y'all soon." He slipped out of the door and my mama reached out to take Karma from me. I'd been trying to prolong the time I was out of my mermaid-cut dress because although it was gorgeous, it wasn't going to be comfortable to wear for more than the half hour I planned to.

"Camille, honey, we have about twenty minutes before its time to walk. Let's go ahead and get into your dress so we can cue you in." My wedding planner Savannah popped up out of nowhere, ushering me toward my dress that was hanging over the closet door. Since my mama and Ca'Mahri had their hands full, Noelle and Savannah helped me to pull my dress over my head. Having it on made things even more real for me, and I was once again sniffling back tears.

They stepped back, giving me a complete view of myself in the full-length mirror, and we all gasped. It was definitely something about a wedding dress that enhanced a woman's looks, and it was doing just that for me. I blinked rapidly and turned side to side, taking myself in.

"Yassss! Now that's a bad bitch! Ayeee!" Noelle instantly hyped me up and I couldn't stop myself from bending over and twerking as much as my dress would allow.

"Ayeee!" Ca'Mahri quickly joined in on the ratchetness. Our antics had everybody amped and our mama had to break it up.

"Ayite, ayite, let's save all that for the reception please!" Groaning, we calmed down and Savannah began getting everybody in order of how they would enter the wedding hall, before disappearing to frantically look for my daddy.

"Hold up, I know y'all gone let an old lady through to see the bride." Ms. Dorothea's voice broke through all the chatter, and everyone moved aside to let her through. Our faces split into smiles as we took each other in, and she nodded in approval. Like everyone in the wedding party, she was clad in a blush pink silk dress that reached her knees and had even gone the extra mile and thrown on a pair of nude kitten heels. "You look so beautiful, baby."

"Thank you, so do you." My lip trembled as she held me at arm's length. Since day one she'd gone out of her way to make this moment happen. Not only had she been the reason we'd met, but her advice and support over the last year and a half had kept us together. I knew that seeing me and Cash get married was something she'd been counting on, and I was happy to make that happen for her.

"I just want you to know I'm so proud of you and my baby Cash. From the moment I saw you, I knew you were the one that was going to change his life for the better, and you're going to make a wonderful wife and granddaughter-in-law, and I can't wait until we share the same name." She embraced me and I held onto her tightly, relishing in the comfort of her arms. "You gone head and get married, baby." Giving my hand a light squeeze, she shuffled aside, making way for Savannah and my dad.

"Okay, let's go maid of honor and bridesmaids!" Savannah called out, directing them out while my daddy wrapped his hand in mine. As I watched them all file out I got choked up, and in an effort to comfort me he rubbed the back of my hand soothingly.

This was it. In the next few minutes, I was going to be marrying the man that had changed my entire life. I damn sure never thought I would've been standing there and as I stood waiting on my cue, it felt like my whole life flashed before my eyes. Sucking my lips into my mouth, I tried to force myself to be still, but that shit wasn't happening.

"Okay honey, you and Mr. Harris will walk out in exactly five minutes," Savannah said, emphasizing her words. I really hadn't realized so much time had passed since she'd first

summoned me, but the five-minute countdown already had
my heart pounding.

"Breath, Camille," my daddy said sternly, giving my hand a
supportive squeeze, and just like that the feeling of anxiety
slowly slipped away. Once we were the last ones in the room,
we paused for thirty seconds before following the same route
that everyone else had. Suddenly it felt like my body was
buzzing as we waited at the back of the church. It was like the
closer I got to Cash the more I excited I became, and I couldn't
wait to marry the nigga that had quickly become my best
friend.

My heart pounded as the beat dropped on Musiq Soul-
child's "Someone," and this time there was no stopping my
tears. Cash had insisted on picking the song I would walk
down the aisle to and I for sure thought he was going to fuck
around and play some drill music. Knowing that he was
playing this especially for me hit different, and I was glad my
veil was down because I was straight up ugly crying at that
point.

I never wanted a woman that wanted
Me for my name or material things
See, I always hoped for a woman that's so sure
Emotionally secure, with spiritual faith
A woman that I can trust with all of my secrets
And even listen to all of my issues
A woman who never judged
Me or how I was
She deals with me strictly through love

I knew my daddy was a big part of the reason why I wasn't
falling on my face as we walked over pink rose petals. The
entire church was bathed in candlelight, and the pews were all

draped in white with pink sashes on the end of each aisle. My eyes briefly rolled over each of my guests before landing on the wedding party...and Cash. I could see it in his eyes that he was just as emotional as me, but was holding it together way better. He was wearing a black tux, with a white shirt and black bowtie, looking so damn handsome with one hand folded over the other in front of him. His dad and brother stood to his side with Kash not too far away from him. Mr. Kendrick patted him on the back proudly, and then whispered something in his ear that had him nodding stiffly and he clenched his jaw. Whatever he said had the tears flowing, and he quickly swiped his face while I dabbed at mine, even though I was sure my makeup was streaking by now.

Someone who will put up with the things
Loving me can bring
But still be there to see us through
Someone who would put up with the
Strange and complicated things
'Cause I would do the same for her too
Someone who I can be real with ain't gotta
Be perfect
'Cause loving one another is all that matters
It's not hard to explain
So believe me when I say
That I found all of that in you

I made it to him just as the chorus ended. My daddy lifted my veil and gave me a quick kiss on the cheek before handing me off to a smiling Cash.

"Amille!" Kash gasped, suddenly realizing that it was me underneath the veil the whole time, sending the church into light laughter. Waving, I blew him a kiss before turning to his daddy. Of course, that nigga looked like he wanted to devour me right there, but he settled for a kiss instead.

"Son, it's not time for that yet," the pastor said, chuckling, and Cash grinned with a shrug.

"My bad, I couldn't help myself."

We looked into each other's eyes as he went on to marry us, and we recited the things we were supposed to say. I was really just following Cash's lead because I was so focused on him, studying his face and occasionally mouthing I love you. When the pastor finally announced us husband and wife, he wasted no time pulling my body into his and kissing me deeply. Hoots and hollers rang out in the church at how steamy it was, but I didn't even care. This was my fucking husband now and I was going to kiss him however I wanted. My life had certainly been changed forever messing around with him, but I wouldn't have changed it for anything.

CHAPTER TWENTY-ONE
CA'MAHRI

I was walking around Camille's reception in search of my nigga as I swatted away multiple hands from touching my baby. Being a new mom had me extremely careful about just anybody holding him and I didn't have any hand sanitizer right then so it was a no for me. My aunt Regine looked like I'd shot her when I turned her ass away and immediately started talking about having changed my diapers, but I walked off. For some reason, Dinero never got the same energy when he told people no about holding DJ, and I was sure it was due to how mean he was. I spotted him in the corner of the room talking to our dads, Snoop, and Cash, who was holding Karma, and I strolled right over. As soon as he laid eyes on the two of us, his face split into a wide grin, and without me having to ask, he scooped his son out of my arms.

"Aye man, you tired of yo' mama?" he asked him, like he wasn't knocked out as usual with his little lips parted. I thought it was cute how he always talked to him, though, and from the way talking had Karma, I knew that it worked. My niece was super smart and Camille was often told that she'd been here before.

"More like Mama tired of him. I'm tryna dance and eat something without his lil' heavy butt weighin' my arm down," I complained even as I placed soft kisses on his curly black hair.

"So, basically you sayin' you brought my son over here so you could shake yo' ass with Noelle and Camille?" He read right through my bullshit, and I couldn't even deny how well he knew me.

With a wide grin, I flashed all thirty-two of my teeth. "Yep!"

"Ohh, all y'all think y'all slick! Camille better chill the fuck out with her married ass!" Cash was already looking around trying to spot her so he could go be a hater, and we all cracked up.

"Aht, aht! Not too much on my sister! You knew what you were signing up for!" I told him as he glowered, looking just like Karma when she didn't get her way. Just like Kash and DJ, our kids had gotten their father's whole faces. It seemed like all me and Camille had done was carry them.

"Yeah, ayite! It's kids up in here, y'all better not!" he fumed, finally giving up the fight to find her in the crowded room.

"I can't make any promises, you know she been hittin' that champagne hard, bro." I continued to fuck with him.

"I know Keisha bet not get her old ass out there! You know her and Allani swear they gon' take over for the 99 and the 2000s!" Kendrick shook his head and cleared the flute of champagne he was drinking before grabbing another off of a passing tray. He was right to be concerned because my mama and Ms. Keisha had already been trying to fuck with the deejay to get him to play some house music.

"Look what you done started now." I rolled my eyes at a grinning Dinero, and he shrugged, looking extremely boyish, even in his grown man tux. He had his bowtie just hanging around his neck, and ever since he'd untied it after the wedding and left it there, I'd been considering pulling him aside. My soon-to-be husband was everything and I'd heard more than a few women talking about him. Usually, I'd be ready to turn up over him, but I completely understood their frustration. Little did they know, I didn't play any games about him and vice versa.

After what happened with Tania, my baby wasn't like his usual self, but he eventually realized he couldn't let it dictate his life. He'd done everything he could do for her and he had to let her go. The birth of our son had helped a lot with that. He felt like he was righting a lot of his wrongs through DJ.

"Nah, this all on you, don't be blamin' me. You lucky I wanted my lil' dude or else you'd be walkin' around holdin' him till this muhfucka over," he said, making me roll my eyes, even though I knew he was dead serious. I feigned an attitude but didn't resist when he slipped an arm around my waist, bringing me closer so he could whisper in my ear, "You look so fuckin' sexy poutin'. Don't make me take you in one of these other rooms." Real shit, I was tempted to keep it up just so he would, but the sound of someone clearing their throat into the microphone snatched everyone's attention.

"Ohhh shit!" all the men said at the same time when we realized it was Noelle, and I couldn't stop a snicker from bubbling up in my throat. My girl was clearly drunk, drunk and swaying from side to side as she looked out over the crowd and held her flute in the air.

"Excuse me, I'd like everybody's attention please." Grumbles sounded around me, but I was fully tuned in to what our bitch was about to say. "I don't know if everybody knows me, but I'm the best friend of Camille and Ca'Mahri and I been here since day one. In fact, I'm the one who told her that her future husband was in one of the patient rooms with his granny. Now they're married with two beautiful kids, and I just need you to know, I'm proud of you, bitch!" This crazy hoe tried to clap as she spoke but was unable to because of the mic and the champagne glass.

"Man, Snoop, get yo' girl, bro!" Cash fussed with his face balled up, and we all looked Snoop's way in shock. As far as we all knew, he could barely stand Noelle, and I didn't know if the look of embarrassment on his face was from being ousted or because she was up there acting a fool.

"I told yo' ass that ain't my girl, nigga!" he huffed, mugging Cash before he walked off, but I peeped it was in the direction of the stage.

"Anyway, it's obvious y'all goin' on to be soccer moms and shit, so I'm gone be the last hot girl of our crew. Y'all just gotta turn up with me every once in a while, and don't be tryna leave me out." She walked from one end of the stage to the other, peering into the crowd like she was looking for us. "Now in honor of y'all hangin' up y'all jerseys, I got a song. Deejay!" she shouted, and the beat dropped for Megan Thee Stallion's "Girls in the Hood" just as Snoop made it to the edge of the stage.

"Fuck bein' good I'ma bad bitch! I'm sick of muhfuckas tryna tell me how to live!"

Every one of the younger women in attendance began singing with her, and I kicked off my shoes, running to meet my sister in the middle of the floor. I didn't know where Camille had come from but by the time I made it in front of the stage, she was already there twerking with everyone else. Noelle's ass even had Ms. Dorothea out there shaking something, but it wasn't long before Snoop finally got ahold of her and the mic. He lifted her into his arms, which didn't stop her from trying to dance, and she grinded against him as he motioned for the deejay to cut it. It took a little bit of time before he finally got the man's attention and he cut the song off, making everybody groan in displeasure.

The music was quickly replaced with some Lucky Daye, completely mellowing out the mood, and I went to walk off the floor only to be swept up by Dinero. I was still trying to catch my breath as he held me and began to sway. "Where's my baby, sir? I know you ain't leave him with nobody so you could come out her and grind on me," I teased, using his own words against him, and he shook his head.

"My mama got him, but I did wanna come over here and grind on you for a lil' bit." We both laughed as he shrugged his shoulders, ready to admit it. Just six months ago I would've been tense at him mentioning his mama, because after our breakup she hadn't been feeling me. It took her a while to come around and a word from Dinero too, but I understood once we had a conversation about why she was being stand-offish toward me. I'd hurt her son like every other woman he'd loved, and Ms. Keisha didn't play about her sons. I was glad that we were able to mend our relationship though. Smiling, I melted into his arms even more as my heart rate slowed down and began blending with his.

"You know I love you, right," I spoke lowly, eyes bucking when he grinned and spun me around before pulling me back against him. "Oh snap, okay!"

"Yeah, a nigga got some moves!" he gloated, letting his hands drop to grip a handful of my ass. "But to answer yo' question, not as much as I love yo' fine ass. You gone be ready to do this all over again in a couple months?" Of course, he was asking about the wedding date that we had set, and if I was being honest, I had been ready. In fact, I slightly regretted not marrying him back in Vegas. Nodding, I looked down at my ten-carat, princess-cut diamond engagement ring.

"I been ready. What about you?" I quizzed, butterflies fluttering in my stomach as I awaited his answer.

"I been ready since I seen yo' lil' crazy ass pull up with a kid holdin' a fuckin' vibrator!" he cracked, and we both fell out laughing. That day had been crazy, but it had put me in the path of the man I was trying to love forever and I wouldn't take it back for anything.

"I mean, sometimes it be like that."

"Naw, it ain't never gon' be like that with me. I got you and DJ forever, no funny shit," he said seriously, looking deeply into my eyes, and I had to say that I believed every word. "I love you, Ca'Mahri soon-to-be Banks."

"I love you too, Dinero." I had to stop myself from crying as a sudden wave of emotion hit me and choked me up. Just a year before I had been ready to give up on the opposite sex, only to fall in thug love with a Chi Town millionaire.

The End.

ALSO BY J. DOMINIQUE

In Thug Love With A Chi-Town Millionaire 2

In Thug Love With A Chi-Town Millionaire

Every Savage Deserves A Hood Chick 2

Every Savage Deserves A Hood Chick

Chino And Chanelle

Chino And Chanelle 2

Chino And Chanelle 3

Giving My Heart To A Chi-Town Menace

Giving My Heart To A Chi-Town Menace: Real & Nova Story

Low Key Fallin' For A Savage

Low Key Fallin' For A Savage 2

Low Key Fallin' For A Savage 3

A Hood Love So Real

A Hood Love So Real 2

The Coldest Savage Stole My Heart

The Coldest Savage Stole My Heart 2

Made in the USA
Columbia, SC
04 September 2024

41624380R00093